TOLIVER'S SECRET

TOLIVER'S SECRET

Esther Wood Brady

illustrated by Richard Cuffari

CROWN PUBLISHERS, INC., NEW YORK

Text copyright © 1976 by Esther Wood Brady
Illustrations copyright © 1976 by Richard Cuffari
Manufactured in the United States of America
Published simultaneously in Canada by General Publishing Company Limited
10 9 8 7 6 5 4 3 2 1

The text of this book is set in 14 pt. Garamond #3.
The illustrations are black and white halftone.

Library of Congress Cataloging in Publication Data

Brady, Esther Wood, 1905–
    Toliver's secret.

    Summary: During the Revolutionary War, a
ten-year-old girl crosses enemy lines to deliver
a loaf of bread containing a message for the
patriots.
    [1. United States—History—Revolution, 1775–
1783—Fiction] I. Cuffari, Richard, 1925–
II. Title.
PZ7.W8484To3   [Fic]   76–15997
ISBN 0–517–52621–2

For Duff

TOLIVER'S SECRET

One

Grandfather must have lost his wits.

Ellen was sure her grandfather had lost his wits when she saw him slip into the dark kitchen and lock the door with a big key. Without giving his usual cheery greeting he tiptoed to the window and pinned the heavy curtains together with a knitting needle.

"Don't want anyone peeping in this morning," he said to Ellen's mother who was making bread on a table by the fireplace.

Lights from a small fire on the hearth darted about

the big old kitchen. From the dark corner where she sat brushing her hair, Ellen could see light glimmering on a tiny silver box he carried in his hand.

"Is the loaf ready now?" Grandfather whispered to her mother.

Mother's white cap fluttered up and down, but she did not speak. Very carefully she patted and shaped a small round loaf of bread.

"Well, then, let us go ahead," Grandfather said as he gingerly placed the silver box on top of the lump of dough.

Ellen stared at the little box. It was his favorite silver snuffbox. She was too surprised to speak when she saw him press the snuffbox into the dough, smooth over the hole that he had made and dust off his hands. His round face had a wide impish smile.

"No one will find it there," he said gleefully. He stepped back and cocked his head to one side. "Bake it crisp and brown, Abby, with a good strong crust. It has a long way to travel."

"You're quite sure no one will find it, Father?" Mother sounded frightened.

"Now don't worry, Abby. No one will find it." He patted her shoulder and gave her a kiss.

Ellen saw that he was wearing the white wig with

the turned-up tail that he always wore when he went to the tavern. Underneath his blue wool coat he wore a long waistcoat with brass buttons down the front. He was short and stout and the buttons marched down his waistcoat in an outward curve. He never wore these clothes when he worked in his barbershop.

Ellen was so puzzled she had to speak up. "Whatever are you planning to do, Grandfather?"

Quickly her grandfather spun around and peered into the deep shadows of the old kitchen. He gave a sharp cry that made her jump up. "I thought you had gone to the corner pump, Ellie!"

Ellen curtsied. "I was just about to make the bed, but I'll leave now, Grandfather." She picked up her red cloak and pulled the hood over her long brown hair.

Grandfather stepped across the room and grasped her by the shoulders. "Don't ever speak of what you have seen, Ellen Toliver," he warned in a gruff voice she had never heard him use before. He was usually so friendly and cheerful, even in the early morning, even with the British officers around. But now his twinkling blue eyes looked as hard as points of steel. Ellen was so startled she dropped her cloak.

"But I was just wondering—"

"Stop. You are no longer a babbling child," he said sharply. "About this you must never talk! Do you hear, Ellen Toliver?"

Ellen nodded. Grandfather wasn't acting like himself at all.

Suddenly, with his usual cheerful smile, he bent down and hugged her to his side. From under his wig she could see some of his sandy red hair peep out around his forehead.

"I must have alarmed you, Ellie—and I am sorry," he said as he kissed her cheek. "But this is something of concern to me—very great concern! And only your mother knows about it. No one else. But now that the three of us know, the three of us must keep it secret."

Ellen nodded. She wasn't sure just what the secret was. But she certainly would not talk about it.

"Sh-h-h-h!" Mother took off her white cap and pushed back a curl that fell across her forehead, leaving a smudge of flour on her brown hair. She cocked her head and listened for a noise upstairs. "Sh-h-h! No telling who might be awake up there."

In the bedrooms upstairs lived six British officers who had moved into Grandfather's house when the redcoats took New York three months ago. Ellen disliked those officers. Always sniffing snuff up their proud noses and sneezing daintily into white kerchiefs when they weren't striding about giving orders.

She hated the way they ordered Mother to bring tea and biscuits to them every morning. But still, they were the masters of the house now. Ellen and her mother curtsied whenever they saw them, and stepped out of their way politely.

"Just pay those redcoats no mind," her grandfather had told them. Sometimes, in the evenings, he would mimic them. He'd take a pinch of snuff from his snuff-box, and with his little finger crooked, he'd put it on the back of his hand and sniff. Then he'd sneeze and sneeze! He'd put his nose in the air very haughtily and dance about the room, flipping up the tails of his coat.

"The Redcoat Minuet," he called the dance. "Come and dance the minuet, dear lady."

Ellen would pick up her skirts and dance with him, holding her hands high, pointing her toes and tossing her head as if she were a Tory lady wearing a big white wig. When they finished the minuet, they'd whirl about the room until they fell back laughing in their chairs to catch their breath. It was fun to do silly things with Grandfather. Ellen's father had never played like this. He had been very serious.

Sometimes Mother would dance, too, pretending a wooden spoon was an ivory fan. It was good to see her laugh after all these months of worry.

Now, in the early morning half-light, Mother pointed up to the ceiling. "Be very quiet," she warned. "Someone may be awake up there and hear us talk about the bread. We must be very cautious."

They stood still and listened. Ellen shivered at the sound of the wind howling over the rooftops, but she heard no stirring of the redcoats upstairs.

"Lazy Lobsterbacks!" grumbled Grandfather. "They're still abed up there. They spend their evenings in the taverns and sleep until noon." Grandfather always got up early and he thought everyone else should too.

For years and years Grandfather Van Horn had been a barber and a wigmaker in the town of New York. Nowadays his shop, in the front part of the house, was filled with British officers who came to have him shave their chins or powder their hair or dress their white wigs. The British officers liked the cheerful little Dutchman.

Ellen watched her grandfather take the wooden bucket from the hearth and look inside. She knew well enough what he would say.

"What a lug-a-bed you are, Ellen. You haven't gone out to the pump yet."

She picked up her red cloak from the floor. "It's because—"

"Don't like snowy mornings, eh?" he teased her. "I may be a stubborn Dutchman, but you know I like the bucket full of water first thing in the morning. Sometimes you're so late I can't wash my face until seven o'clock."

"I'll save water for you to wash your face, Father," Mother said hastily. "Ellen is just slow to get started in the mornings. I know how she feels."

"Slow!" cried Grandfather. "She's like a turtle! It seems to take her an hour to come back from the pump. I used to buy water from the drayman, but I thought it was good for Ellen to go out. She stays indoors too much."

Mother's eyes were anxious. Her face was so thin now, it made her eyes look huge. "I hope you'll excuse her, Father," she began slowly as she tightened the knot of brown hair at her neck. "She's not used to this town yet—living quiet as we always did in our little village. We've been here scarce a month and it takes time to get used to different ways."

"Nonsense!" said Grandfather. He poured the last of the water into a mug and handed the bucket to Ellen.

Perhaps she should tell him why she was late every day. She knew he would think it was not very important. But it was important! To her, it was!

"I'm late because of that tough Dicey at the pump," she said.

"What's a dicey?" asked Grandfather.

"Dicey's a girl. Everyone is afraid of her. She says she's going to wring my neck and I think she means it, too."

"Is that the way she talks to you, Ellen?" Mother asked.

Whenever Ellen thought of Dicey, she could almost hear her rowdy laughter. It gave her a hollow feeling in the pit of her stomach. "She screams at me and I have to go to another pump farther away."

"Fiddlesticks!" said Grandfather. "Just stand up for yourself, Ellen. That's what I did—when I was a boy and small for my age."

Ellen doubted she could stand up for herself when Dicey went blustering about like a tough butcher-boy.

"Ellen's not a boy," Mother said quietly. "She can't roister about like a boy."

"Oh, Double Fiddlesticks!" said Grandfather impatiently. "She could talk back to that little girl at the pump."

"Dicey's not a little girl," Ellen protested. "She's bigger than I am and she's mean."

"Talk back to her anyway, Ellen," Grandfather urged her. "Don't be so meek and mild."

Mother seldom spoke sharply to anyone, but now she folded her arms and looked at Grandfather. "Her father wanted Ellen to be ladylike," she said. "You remember my husband was a schoolmaster, college educated. He knew all about training children."

"Yes, I suppose he did," said Grandfather.

"Indeed he did," Abby said firmly. "He was very pleased with Ellen's quiet ways and her pretty manners."

Grandfather looked puzzled as he watched her put the loaf of bread on a long-handled shovel. It was plain to see that he didn't understand his daughter. She looked so much like him—and yet they were so different. "Well, Abby," he said, "your husband was a good man, a very good man indeed. But," he reminded her, "Ellen can have pretty manners and still be bold when she needs to be. She can learn to stand up for herself!"

"Not like a boy," Ellen repeated her mother's words. "You know I can't fight back like a boy!"

"You don't have to fight back with your fists," said Grandfather impatiently. "Use your brains, Ellen. You're a smart girl. Bluff her. Stare her down. Get your friends to join you and chase away the bully."

"I just don't see how I could do that," Ellen said. Her big brother, Ezra, often said to her, "Don't be so scared, Ellie. Just talk back to people. You're too polite—or timid—or something." Ezra was a care-free boy with auburn hair and a wide smile—like Grandfather's. He'd talk back to anyone—even the captain of the village militia.

"Well," said Grandfather, "you're a smart girl. You'll think of a way."

Now that the oven at the back of the fireplace was hot, Mother raked out the coals and slid in two long loaves of bread. She took a last look at the mysterious round one before slipping it in too.

Grandfather unlocked the kitchen door and went into his shop at the front of the house. The tail of his wig turned up jauntily as he straightened his coat and picked up his cane.

"Why in the world did Grandfather put his snuff-box in that loaf of bread?" Ellen whispered.

"Best not to ask any questions, Ellen," Mother said.

Grandfather came back to the door of the kitchen and winked at Ellen. "Just go and stand up to that Dicey," he urged her. "You have more of your Grandfather's spirit than you think, Ellen. And now, Abby, I'm going to the Tavern for breakfast. And to hear the news. I'll be back when the bread is baked." He glanced up at the little square clock that hung on the wall of his shop with its pendulum swinging slowly back and forth. "You remember the shop is closed for the day," he reminded her. "I've given my shaver a holiday."

The young man, Alexander, who lived in the attic and who helped Grandfather in the shop while he learned to be a barber, had gone off last night to visit his family.

Grandfather gave Ellen a big smile. "That girl, Dicey, sounds like a bully," he said. "She'll back down if you just stand up for yourself."

Ellen wasn't so sure of that. It may have been true when Grandfather was a boy, but she knew it wouldn't work now, with a tough girl like Dicey.

Two

Ellen dreaded that trip to the pump. It would be good to stay in the safe warm kitchen and never go out.

A crackling fire on the hearth made bright lights on the copper pans and on the blue china plates in the cupboard. It made the quilt on the big bed look like a field of bluebells and shone on the bunches of dried herbs that hung from the shadowy rafters overhead.

Ellen looked around. "This kitchen makes me feel

happy," she said.

"It makes me happy, too," Mother said wistfully. "I used to sew and knit with my mother here by the fire. She taught me my lessons here at this big table by this very window."

On the table was a basket of clay curlers and combs and brushes as well as a wigstand covered with a net and a half-made wig. White hair spilled from a wooden box.

"We used to sit here and curl and dress the wigs for my father's customers. And help him make some of the wigs, too," Mother added.

"And now you and I dress the wigs for the redcoat officers," said Ellen.

"Yes," said Mother sadly. "Here we are curling wigs for the soldiers who have come to defeat us. And there's not much you and I can do about it. These are terrible mixed-up times, Ellen."

Ellen knew that well enough. Ever since the British army came to New York last summer. She remembered the night in August when the alarm had come to their village. The British had landed on Long Island!

Her father's thin face had been grim when he locked up his schoolhouse and rushed off with his musket to join the other men in the village militia.

That very night the militia had marched off to Brooklyn Heights to help General Washington's army defend Long Island and New York. In spite of all her mother's pleading, Ezra went with him. He was only fifteen, but he could shoot as well as a man. "We'll send those cutthroats back to old King George," he had boasted.

Everyone knew the brave Patriots could drive the British out. Washington had driven them out of Boston last year, hadn't he?

But the British had three times as many men as Washington had—and all of them well trained in war. They defeated him at Brooklyn Heights and they captured New York City. They drove his army north and in November captured Fort Washington, where they took three thousand prisoners. People heard the news in stunned surprise.

Then the British took Fort Lee across Hudson's River with all of Washington's cannon. And finally they sent what was left of his army scurrying across New Jersey. The colonists could hardly believe such news. They had felt so sure that courage and the will to win would be enough to beat back the British.

"Where do you think Ezra is today, Mother?"

Immediately Ellen was sorry she had asked, for Mother bit her lip and was silent.

"Only the good Lord knows," she said at last. "If he's alive—and isn't on a prison ship, he must have gone to Pennsylvania with Washington's army."

Ellen knew that asking about Ezra had reminded her mother of the other news that had come to them after the Battle of Brooklyn Heights. Her father had been killed. Many men from their village had been killed that day.

She and her mother had been all alone. Mother was nervous and upset most of the time and worried about what to do.

When at last they had no more food in their storeroom—and no money to buy anything—and the November days were growing bitter cold, Mother had said, "Our neighbors can't help us, for they have as much hardship as we. There is nothing to do but to go back to my father, Ellie. Even if the town is in the hands of the enemy now."

"How can we travel, Mother?" Ellen had asked.

"We must walk! There's naught else to be done!"

And so they had walked ten miles back to New York. Grandfather had welcomed them joyfully and had given them the big kitchen to live in while he slept on a couch in his shop. The rest of his house was already occupied by British officers.

"Now remember, Ellen," Mother had said, "we must be very careful here. Most of the people who have stayed in New York are friends of the British and want them to win the war. Not Grandfather, of course, nor any of his friends. Those of us who are Patriots, here in town, must lie low."

"Just like rabbits in a rabbit hole," Ellen suggested.

Mother shrugged her shoulders and sighed. "Well, rabbits know how to act when the enemy is all around them."

"And I suppose even rabbits need water," Ellen grumbled aloud to herself.

No longer able to put off the trip to the pump, she pulled on her stout leather shoes and picked up her red cloak. It was a good warm cloak that her mother had made, and it hung almost to the hem of her long wool dress. To stay safe indoors all winter would make her very happy. But of course, since the wooden bucket was quite empty there was nothing to do but pull her cloak around her, cover her head with the hood and start. She took a long breath. If she went very slowly she might find that Dicey had gone home.

"Just go to another pump, Ellen, if Dicey bothers you," her mother said. "Don't go asking for trouble."

Walking slowly through the barbershop Ellen passed the counter that ran along the wall. On the counter were five china wigstands with painted gentlemen's faces beneath fancy white wigs. They looked, Ellen thought, as if they were smirking at her.

"Smiling like idiots," she said. "And you don't even see that jar of leeches there beside you." The dark slimy little worms lay quietly in the water that filled a big green jar. Barbers always had leeches handy to put on bruises and swellings. Ellen found them almost too horrible to look at.

From the kitchen she heard her mother call after her. "Mind the slippery steps, Ellen. And don't talk to strangers!"

Mother always said that—every time she went out. And Ellen never talked to strangers! It seemed to Ellen that Mother worried about everything.

With great care Ellen crept down the icy steps of the barbershop and out into the street. The air smelled of winter—snow and sweet wood smoke mixed together. It was only half light in the early morning, but already the apprentices were sweeping the steps of the shops and brushing the snow from the signs overhead.

As nimbly as she could, she dodged out of the way of carts and wagons that rumbled along slowly while their horses slipped and slid on the icy cobblestones. It seemed to her that every man with a wheelbarrow barked at her to get out of his way. And every workman with a load on his shoulders seemed to give her a shove. People were cross on a nipping cold morning.

When she walked with Grandfather on Sunday afternoons, things were different, for he was friends with almost everyone in the neighborhood. Even when they walked down to the Battery or out Bowery Lane to the country, he always stopped to chat with friends.

"Jump aside!" shouted three girls as they sloshed along with full water buckets. Ellen hopped out of their way. Just in time to get hit by a snowball. Across the street the Brinkerhoff boys were knocking icicles down from the roof with snowballs. They hurled several at her, but she pretended not to notice.

She had not even reached the corner when a tall thin man with a tallow-spattered apron shouted at her roughly. "Look sharp now, girl!" he roared as he pulled her against the wall, knocking her bucket from her hand and spilling his own baskets of candles. Down the busy street dashed three officers on big black horses. Without a glance to either side, they rode as if they owned the whole world.

"Drat those redcoats!" muttered the candlemaker. "The lordly way they push us around!" He knelt down to gather up his candles. "Did I hurt you, girl?"

"No, sir," said Ellen politely. She began to help him pick up his candles. The more she delayed, the more chance there was that Dicey might have gone home by the time she reached the pump.

The neighborhood pump was only two blocks away, although it seemed like a mile to Ellen. As she came near, she could hear the old wooden handle creak and groan. A group of women and girls were waiting in line to fill their buckets. They huddled in their shawls, and stamped their feet to keep warm. Ellen looked cautiously to see whether Dicey was there before she took her place at the end of the line.

The women were talking about the same thing they talked about every morning. High prices! The high price of wool—the high price of firewood—the high price of cornmeal and flour and mutton. That kind of talk made Ellen worry about eating anything at all.

"Has Dicey been here this morning?" she asked the woman ahead of her. She was an old woman with a work-worn face, dressed in a man's coat instead of a shawl.

"She's gone home, I reckon," muttered the woman.

"That's good." Ellen heaved a sigh of relief as she pulled her red cloak about her. "I was hoping she wouldn't be here."

"What a mean one she is!" said the woman. "She seems to get pleasure out of pestering them that's smaller."

"She always pesters me, and I don't know why."

"She likes to see you run. I think she likes to make you go to another pump."

"But I never bother her at all! Why would she want me to go to another pump?"

The woman cocked her head to one side and looked at Ellen. "Maybe because you're pretty and look well cared for, and she ain't."

Pretty! Ellen was surprised to hear that. With her straight brown hair! And her face as pale as tallow! Ezra sometimes teased her and said she looked like a burned-out candle. Mother, of course, told her she was pretty, but her father only said, "Don't make her vain. A good character is better than a pretty face."

Just at that moment there was a great commotion as Dicey came around the corner. She was dragging little Arnie Brinkerhoff, holding him firmly by the ear as he squirmed and tried to get away.

"Don't you throw snowballs at me!" Dicey shouted at him.

Dicey's chapped cheeks were as red and rough as her flannel petticoat, and her eyes made Ellen think of a pig. She looked like a bold scrawny public pig dressed up in a drooping wool skirt. Her pale hair was uncombed and blowing in the wind like a dirty handkerchief.

"Let me go!" Arnie screeched. "I'm sorry! I'm sorry, Dicey!"

"Don't you do that again," Dicey warned him as she let him go with a shove. She brushed the snow from her chest and looked up and down the line of laughing people.

When she saw Ellen she put her hands on her hips, spread her feet wide and cried, "You trying to come here again, Wooden Doll? I told you not to come back here."

"Now just stand up to her," Ellen said to herself. But she could feel her feet backing away.

Bending down, the woman in the man's coat whispered to Ellen. "Just pay her no mind when she tries to scare you. Don't look at her."

Ellen looked off across the street, but Dicey kept right on yelling. "Look at the little baby in her red cloak." She shoved her face in front of Ellen. "Afraid to look at me, aren't you?" she jeered. "Too scared to say a word."

"Leave me alone," said Ellen. "I didn't hurt you."

Dicey's face was red with anger and her little eyes were closed in slits as she sneered at Ellen. "Why don't you bring your mamma along if you're so scared?"

"Here now," said the woman in the man's coat as she stepped between them. "Just leave the girl alone."

At that Dicey's rough hands grabbed Ellen's bucket and threw it into the street—banging and bumping across the cobblestones.

"Get your water out of the gutter," she cried.

Ellen turned and ran. She could hear Dicey call after her, "And don't come here again!"

Ellen scurried across the street and hid behind a wooden cart. She hated herself for running, but she could not make her feet stop. She could hear Dicey's taunting laughter, "Don't you come back here, putting on your fine airs."

26

A workman with a load of kindling on his back kicked her bucket out of his way. Ellen scrambled in the gutter to get it and set off for the pump two blocks farther away. She was so angry she stomped along, kicking at the stones in the street and hurting her toes.

"I wish I could be invisible," she said to herself. "I wish I could watch everything and nobody could see me."

At the second pump she took her place in line. Even here a little old man was grumbling about the high price of firewood, and the women talked about the high price of flour and wool and mutton. Always the same talk.

When it was her turn, Ellen pumped the wooden handle until her bucket was brimming with icy cold water. It was heavy, but she knew that if she carried home a half bucket she would only have to come back —and run the risk of meeting Dicey again.

On the way home she saw the man who sold water from the Tea-Water Pump. His horse pulled a great round cask on wheels. "Good pure water!" he called. "Good pure water for your tea. The best water in town." Ellen knew it was the best water in town, but it came from a well that was too far away for them to

carry buckets home. Grandfather said he used to buy the man's water, but now he thought it was good for Ellen to go out.

"Good for me to go out!" thought Ellen scornfully. "Someday I'm going to stay at home all the time and never go out!"

When she reached the steps of the shop, she could see Grandfather coming toward her, hopping on one foot while two carpenters in leather aprons helped him. To her surprise she saw that he had lost his hat and his wig had fallen down over his eyes. He looked terrible.

Quickly Ellen put down her bucket and ran to meet him. "What happened, Grandfather? Did you fall on the ice?"

Grandfather looked angry—and very worried, too. "Aye, I fell on the ice," he groaned. "If it hadn't been for my wig and my hat I would have knocked myself senseless."

One of the carpenters tried to comfort him. "Don't concern yourself, Mr. Van Horn. We'll make you a crutch."

But Grandfather only barked at him. "Better make me a new leg. That's what I need." He closed his eyes and moaned while the two men helped him up the steps.

The door of the shop was flung open as Mother held out her arms to help him in. "What has happened to you, Father?" she said in a distressed voice.

"I've sprained my ankle," Grandfather said to her. "I can't walk at all. And what's to be done now, Abby? What's to be done now?"

Three

Ellen lugged her bucket up the steps and followed her grandfather into the shop. As he crossed the room and flopped down on his couch he looked like a rooster with a broken leg whose top feathers had fallen over his beak.

"This will make you more comfortable," Mother said, tucking a pillow under his head and spreading a wool blanket over him.

"Best keep him off that foot for a while," said one of the carpenters. "I'll make a crutch for him and bring it round in a day or two."

At that suggestion Grandfather groaned. "No crutch. I won't use a crutch. I'll get well before you can make it." He pushed his wig off his head and ran his fingers through his short reddish hair. "Today of all days," he said.

Mother thanked the carpenters for bringing him home and shut the door firmly after them. Then she walked to the door that blocked off the stairway to the bedrooms above and made sure it was shut, too.

"Now don't excite yourself, Father," she whispered. "I know you'll think of something."

"But they leave at eleven!" cried Grandfather.

"Sh-h-h-h, just stay calm."

Ellen wondered what was going on as she got an earthen pot from the cupboard. Grandfather seemed so worried, and there was the strange loaf of bread with the snuffbox baked inside.

She poured half the water from the bucket into the pot and brought it to her grandfather's couch. She watched him pull off his shoe and white stocking and wince as his foot hit the cold water.

She picked up his wig that had fallen to the floor. Sitting down on the couch, she stroked his sandy red hair. It was hard to see Grandfather lying there all disheveled. With his leg hanging over the side of the couch and his foot in a pot of water, he looked like Ezra. Ezra was always getting into some kind of trouble—when he fell from a tree or got caught in a beaver trap.

But never Grandfather. He was the one who took care of everyone else. He'd put leeches on a bruise or cut a vein and let the blood flow out into a basin to cure an ailment. Everyone came to him with their troubles. Ellen hated to see him look worried. The freckles stood out on his anxious face as clearly as spots of rust.

"Would you like some hot porridge, Grandfather?" she asked.

"No, thank you, Ellen," said Grandfather without opening his eyes. "What time is it?"

Ellen looked up at the little square clock.

"It's only eight o'clock. Would you like some tea?" she asked eagerly. "I could take a few of the officers' tea leaves from the tea caddy."

"No," Grandfather said again as he pulled his foot from the water and held it up to look at it. With a groan he let it fall back on the couch. There was no doubt about it, the ankle was even bigger than when he first came home.

If it were someone else's ankle Grandfather would put on leeches to take out that swelling, Ellen thought. Now she knew what she had to do. She'd put the leeches on his ankle for him. She'd take the tongs and put those slimy leeches on his ankle, watching them slither around until they got a grip on the skin. Then she'd have to see them swell up while they sucked out the blood. She shuddered at the thought, but she'd do anything to help Grandfather get better.

Though it made her feel sick to think of it, she stood up and looked at the green glass jar on the counter. Once again it seemed to her that the painted faces of the wig gentlemen were smirking at her beneath their big white wigs. "Pox on you," she said to them although they really hadn't laughed at her. "I can make myself do it."

Gingerly she picked up the jar with both hands and turned to Grandfather who lay with his eyes closed.

"Look, Grandfather," she whispered, "I can help you. Take your foot out of the water and I'll put some leeches on it."

Grandfather opened his eyes and smiled at her weakly. "Thank you, Ellie," he murmured, "but it isn't time for the leeches yet. Later—when it's black and blue." He patted her waist. "That was kind of you."

She put the jar back on the counter and hastily wiped her hands on her skirt. She saw how really tired Grandfather was and drew the curtains across the two front windows to shut out the noises of the street. Since that made the room dark she gathered pine knots from a basket to start a fire in the small fireplace. Perhaps Grandfather would feel more cheerful when he could look at a bright fire across the room.

As she sat down in the chair by the fire to eat the porridge her mother brought her, Ellen could see that Grandfather had dozed off with his arms across his face. He lay so still and quiet that the ticking of the clock sounded very loud in the room. In the street she could hear the creaking of an old oxcart and then the quick jingling bells of a sleigh. But inside there was only silence.

Suddenly Grandfather cleared his throat and called out crossly, "Where's that boy Ezra? Didn't he come back to New York with you?"

With her spoon halfway to her mouth, Ellen turned and stared at him. Had he forgotten about Ezra? He must be out of his head!

"Ezra didn't come back with us," Ellen reminded

him. "He marched away with General Washington's army last fall. Don't you remember?"

Grandfather clapped his hands to his head. "My brains are addled. Must be from the fall on the ice."

When at last Mother pulled the brown loaves from the oven, the whole house was filled with the smell of fresh-baked bread. She brought the round loaf to show Grandfather what a fine strong crust it had.

To Ellen's surprise Grandfather groaned again when he saw it. "Put it there on the shelf," he said. "But what's to be done now?" Ellen heard him whisper. "This message must get there tomorrow."

"Couldn't your friend, the cobbler, take it for you?" Mother asked in a low voice.

"He went last week, and they are suspicious of him."

Ellen could see her mother's nervous hands playing with the scissors and the razors on the little table between the two chairs. "Perhaps—maybe I could take it for you, Father," she said softly. "I could dress up as a man."

"You'd fool no one but an idiot, Abby. You'd never get home again."

Grandfather's fingers played up and down the row of brass buttons on his vest. "A barber is welcome anywhere. That's how I went through their lines before—with my shaving kit and my jar of leeches."

So Grandfather must be some kind of spy, Ellen thought with alarm. There must be a message in that loaf of bread and he must have planned to take it through the enemy lines today. He had said something about leaving at eleven.

As she sat there, Ellen had the feeling that her Grandfather was staring at her. She could almost feel his eyes go through her.

"Ellen could take it for me!" he said with decision.

Ellen could not believe she had heard her Grandfather correctly. He couldn't mean that he'd send her through enemy lines as a spy.

Mother sank down on one of the barber chairs by the counter and stared at him in startled surprise. "A little girl! To do a man's work!"

"She's ten, isn't she? Almost eleven! She's old enough."

"But, Father!" Mother cried. She was almost stuttering in her hurry to object to Grandfather's idea. "It's too cold to go sailing across the Bay . . . in December . . . a little girl would freeze with only a shawl to wear!" She clapped her hands to her brown hair and ruffled it with nervous fingers. "How could you think of a thing like that?"

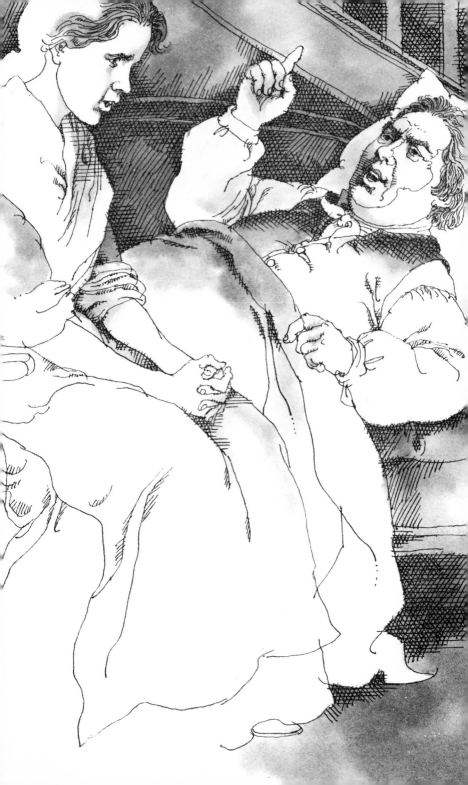

"Now don't get so upset, Abby," Grandfather whispered. "She could wear Ezra's old clothes to keep warm. No one would notice a small boy with a loaf of bread."

Quickly Ellen looked from one to the other. Her mother wouldn't let him go ahead with a scheme so wild.

Mother's blue eyes flashed. "But Ellen doesn't even look like a boy."

"Sh-h-h," said Grandfather, pointing to the ceiling. "We could cut her hair like a boy's." He seemed rather pleased with the idea of the disguise.

"Just like that!" said Mother. "You expect me to cut my daughter's hair and send her off just like that! You forget, Father, I gave my husband to the cause of freedom and my son has gone to the war, too. I won't let you send my little girl."

Grandfather was surprised by this outburst. "But she isn't going to the *war*," he said gently. "All she has to do is cross over to Elizabeth-town on an oyster-man's boat, and hand the loaf of bread to my friend Shannon. And come home again."

Mother threw up her hands. "It's too dangerous," she protested. She set her mouth in a stubborn line as she shook her head. "It's just too risky."

40

Ellen looked from one to the other. Grandfather couldn't be serious about this. She couldn't pretend she was a boy. She was too small and she wouldn't know how to act. Maybe someone like Dicey could do it. But Grandfather was looking right at her.

"I couldn't do it, Grandfather," she stammered. "Why, I don't even know where Elizabeth-town is. And I don't know Mr. Shannon. How could I find a man I don't know?" In her fright she was tripping over her words. "How could I go on an oysterman's boat by myself?"

Leaning on his elbow Grandfather beckoned her to his couch. "Look, Ellen Toliver," he said quietly, "I wouldn't send you off to do something that was dangerous. I love you too much for that. Now, it might take courage for you to sail across the Bay. But it isn't dangerous."

"But I'd be too scared to do a thing like that by myself," Ellen protested. "You know how scared I get. I just can't do the hard things you tell me to do. You think I'm like Ezra, but I'm not, Grandfather. I can't even stand up to Dicey." She hated to tell him that she had run away from Dicey again in spite of all he had told her this morning.

She kept her head down so he couldn't see her eyes.

"I don't have courage like other people. Ezra says I haven't any at all."

"I don't agree with you," said Grandfather. "You had courage when you and your mother walked ten miles to New York," he reminded her.

"And you had courage when you two stayed all alone in your house with war all around you."

Ellen nodded.

"And today when you brought the leeches to put on my ankle. That took courage, didn't it?"

Well, yes, thought Ellen, that did take courage, but it wasn't the same as going across the Bay all alone to a place she'd never been.

"We get over fear," said Grandfather, "by doing things we think we cannot do. These are trying times, Ellen. Many people are doing things they thought they never could do."

It was hard to think of an answer. Ellen stood twisting her fingers and wondering what to say. She thought if they made her go, she'd never get back again.

Four

"I will explain to you what this is all about," said Grandfather, "and then you can decide what to do, Ellen. I hear a lot of talk among the British officers in my shop. I hear a lot in the Tavern, too. I have information that must get to General Washington by tomorrow night at the latest. It must get there without fail. That's why I have hidden it in a loaf of bread. The bread won't attract attention, and it can be passed from one messenger to another until it gets to head-quarters."

With a frown on her face, Mother jumped up from her chair and stood in front of him. "How could a message be that important, now?" she protested. "It is only two weeks until Christmas! And the officers are planning to stop the war for Christmas. I know they are."

Grandfather scowled at her. "And how could you know that, pray tell?"

"Why," said Mother, "people all over New York are having parties and balls for the officers. I hear that hundreds of fruitcakes have been made already—and thousands of candles. That's what I heard when I went to the candle shop."

Grandfather shook his head. His face, usually so pink cheeked and jolly, looked gray and drawn.

"And General Howe loves parties," Mother pressed on eagerly. "They all love parties. I know there won't be any fighting at Christmastime!"

Grandfather's eyes were grim. "Nevertheless, this message is very important! Our army has been defeated time and time again for months!" He pulled his foot from the pot of water and sat up. "Why," he exclaimed, "the British brought thirty thousand men—three times as many as Washington had!" He swung his leg over the side of the couch as if, in his eagerness to do something for Washington's army, he was ready to start.

"Whatever information we Patriots here in New York can send him about the British is important! The only way we can win is by using surprise and cunning and determination." He started to get up, but his foot touched the floor, and he groaned and fell back on the couch.

He looked at Ellen intently. "Can you understand what I have been telling you?"

"I think so."

Ellen could see that Grandfather was very serious about the need to send his message. She, too, had been worried about all the news of lost battles and retreats, especially since Ezra was with that army. She remembered how joyous everyone had been last July when they heard about the Declaration of Independence. There had been bonfires on the village green and singing and dancing in the streets. And then the British army came to New York and there had been three months of defeat.

"If you understand how important it is to take the message, Ellen, I'll tell you how it can be done. And then you are to decide."

Ellen listened and didn't say a word.

"You walk down to the docks near the Market-house and get on a farmer's boat—or an oysterman's. They come over early every morning and they go back to Elizabeth-town at eleven o'clock. Elizabeth is a very small town. When you get off the boat, you'll find the Jolly Fox Tavern without any trouble. My good friend Mr. Shannon runs the tavern, and you give the loaf of bread to him. That's all there is for you to do, Ellen. The Shannons will welcome you and take good care of you."

Sailing across the Bay didn't seem so hard. It was finding a boat here in New York and asking a stranger for a ride that worried her.

"How could I find the right boat to take me?" she asked. She didn't intend to go, but she thought she'd ask anyway.

"The docks are right near Front Street where we walked on Sunday afternoon. The farmers and the oystermen tie up their boats near the Market-house. They are friendly people and they often take passengers back to Elizabeth-town since the ferryboat stopped running. I'll give you money to pay."

"And how would I get home again—if I should decide to go?" she said in a very low voice.

"Oh, the Shannons will put you on a boat early in the morning. You'll be back here by ten o'clock."

"Does Mr. Shannon take the bread to General Washington?" she asked.

"No, he takes it to a courier who will ride part of the way. Then he'll give it to another courier who will ride through the night with it. And finally a third man will carry it to the General in Pennsylvania."

Ellen thought about the messengers riding alone through the countryside to carry the secret message. She wondered how it felt to be all alone among the British soldiers.

Mother interrupted. "It's too much to ask of her, Father. She's only ten."

Her father reached out and squeezed her hand. "Abby, dear," he said, "I know you are distressed because of all that has happened this fall. But don't make the child timid. We all have to learn to do things that seem hard at first. A child can't start too early to learn that."

Ellen knew her grandfather wouldn't send her if he thought she couldn't do it. Now that she thought it over she knew that if she walked carefully she could remember the way to Front Street. And she would have money to pay for the boat. She had liked sailing across the East River when she and Mother had taken the ferryboat from Brooklyn to New York last November. Perhaps it wouldn't be too hard. "But what would I do if I got lost?"

"If you lose your way, just speak up and ask someone for directions," said Grandfather.

"You're sure there is no one else to take it for you, Grandfather?"

"With this bad ankle I can't walk around New York to find one of my friends—and I wouldn't know where to send you or your mother to look. Besides, there isn't time. I need your help, Ellen."

Ellen was quiet for a long time.

"Very well," she said finally. "I'll do it—if you are really sure I can."

"I know you can, Ellen. And Abby," he said, "this is nothing too hard for a child of ten. The Shannons will take good care of her, you may be sure of that. In that chest in the kitchen are clothes that Ezra left here years ago. Go out and see what you find, Ellen."

Now that she had decided to go, Ellen ran quickly to the kitchen and poked around among the blankets and old clothes in the chest that sat near the fireplace. She was eager to see what was there. "Here's a striped cap," she exclaimed. "And here's that old blue jacket with the holes in the elbows. I remember these brass buttons." Grandfather had bought Ezra all new clothes when he had come to New York to visit several years ago.

Ellen put on a red knitted shirt that was too small and the blue wool jacket that was too big. The brass buttons made her think of Ezra's grin. She put on heavy gray stockings before she pulled up the short breeches. The leather breeches were so old and stiff they could almost stand alone. She kicked up her legs to make them soften up.

Not since she was a small child had she known what fun it was to kick her legs as high as she could. She tried to kick the skillet that hung beside the fireplace.

"These will be better for walking than petticoats," she said as she pranced about the kitchen. "Why can't girls wear these, too?"

"Ellen Toliver," said her mother primly. "It would be unseemly."

After trying on Ezra's boots, which were too big for her, she decided she would wear her own leather shoes to make walking easier. Certainly it would be easier to jump out of the way of horses and wheelbarrows and it would be better for climbing on the boat.

She ran into the shop to show her grandfather how she looked. For the first time since he fell on the ice,

Grandfather laughed. "You look like a ragged little urchin all right," he said, "with those holes in your elbows. But all the better. No one will even notice you. And now we must cut your hair."

Mother picked up the scissors and stroked Ellen's long brown hair. "Couldn't we just tuck her hair under the cap?" she asked.

"No," said Ellen firmly. "I might forget and take it off! That would be dreadful. Besides, it might look bunchy beneath a cap." Better to have it short and not worry about it. She remembered her friend Lucinda who had short hair with a band of ribbon around her head. Lucinda looked very pretty with short hair. "Cut it off!" she said impatiently.

Grandfather smiled from his couch. "You'll do right well, Ellen," he said. "Tie a pigtail in back with a cord and then just snip off the part that is too long."

Ellen could feel her mother's hands tremble as she tied back the hair and snipped at the long pigtail.

"It will grow back," Ellen said to her. "How do I look?" Jumping up from the chair she stepped over the hair on the floor and stared at herself in the mirror.

"Why, I favor my father with my hair tied back!" she exclaimed. Her brown eyes were just like her father's eyes although not stern like his. Her face was thin like his, too. She stared at herself. Suddenly the person staring back at her didn't look like Ellen Toliver, and for a minute it frightened her to look so changed. Glancing sideways she could see her grandfather smiling his old cheerful smile.

Mother had given him the loaf of bread which he was wrapping in a blue kerchief and tying with a good strong knot.

"Where shall I hide the bread?" Ellen asked him.

"Don't hide it," he told her. "Don't think of hiding it. Just go along swinging this blue bundle as if it were nothing at all. There is only one thing to be careful about, Ellen. Be sure you give the bread to no one but Mr. Shannon."

His eyes grew as hard as they had been earlier that morning, when she surprised him in the kitchen. "No one but Mr. Shannon. He and I might hang if we were caught."

"Hang!" cried Ellen. "You mean on a gallows tree?"

Ellen's hands trembled so that she could hardly button the brass buttons on her jacket. No one had mentioned hanging before. If she had known her grandfather might hang she never would have agreed to do it. It wasn't fair. She gulped and at last the words came out. "I can't do it, Grandfather. I just can't. I'm too scared and I might make a mistake."

"You can do it, Ellen. Better than anyone else. No one in the world will suspect a loaf of bread in the hands of a child. If, perchance, someone found the message in the bread, just act surprised and say you don't know a thing about it!" He smiled at her to encourage her. "Just hang onto the bread good and tight until you see Mr. Shannon. That won't be hard to do, now will it?"

"But don't talk to any strangers, Ellie," Mother pleaded.

"Now, Abby. She has common sense."

"You're sure I won't make a mistake, Grandfather?"

"I can't see where you could go wrong, Ellen. The boatmen are kindly and they take people every day. And at the other end of the trip are my good friends the Shannons."

"Well, then," she said. "I think I am all ready now."

"Good!" cried Grandfather. "When you hand the bread to Mr. Shannon say this to him, 'I have brought you a present for your birthday.' He will understand what it means."

Mother slipped two corncakes into her pocket. "You'll get hungry before you get there, I'm sure." She was trying hard to sound cheerful. "I've always heard about Mistress Shannon's good potpies, and now you can eat one."

Grandfather slipped some coins into her pocket. Then he squeezed her hand until it hurt.

"God bless you, Ellen. I'm proud of you."

Mother pulled the red and white striped cap down around her ears and gave her a pair of mittens as well as a hug that almost smothered her. Then she stepped to the door and opened it. "I think you are a brave girl, Ellen."

Ellen stood at the top of the steps and looked up and down the street. She took a deep breath. Mother had said she was brave and Grandfather had said he was proud of her—well, she hoped they were right.

Five

At first it felt strange to be walking down the same old street, looking like someone else. Ellen was sure people were watching her and wondering why she was dressed as a boy. What should she say if a woman walked up to her and asked, "Why is a girl wearing those clothes? It's not very seemly to show your legs." She'd pretend the woman had mistaken her for someone else.

But after a while, in Ezra's old breeches, her legs free of skirts and petticoats, she found it was fun to stomp along the cobblestones. She forgot what people might say. It was fun to dodge the oxcarts and the wheelbarrows and run against the wind with no cloak to hold her back. No one noticed her at all.

When she came to the pump corner she saw that Dicey and the two Brinkerhoff boys were having a snowball fight.

"That's a fair match," Ellen said to herself. She turned her head so Dicey could not see her. "Let them fight it out."

But she knew Dicey had seen her when she heard her call out, "Stop!" Ellen's heart almost stood still.

"New boy!" Dicey called. "What's your name?"

Why, Dicey didn't know her! It was just like being invisible. Dicey had looked at her and didn't know her.

Ellen peeped over her shoulder just in time to see Aaron Brinkerhoff push Dicey against a tree trunk and hold her there while Arnie gleefully scrubbed her face with handfuls of snow.

"Stop!" screamed Dicey. "Stop! Two against one ain't fair." She kicked and twisted away from them. Then, to Ellen's surprise, Dicey turned and ran away, crying like a bawling calf. Ellen stood and stared at her. For a moment she even felt sorry for her.

"Well, at least she didn't know me," Ellen said to

herself. "I feel invisible."

"I'm invisible, I'm invisible," she kept saying as she ran happily down the street. Already she felt better about making the trip.

And then she felt a whack on her back that sent her spinning across the slippery cobblestones. The blue kerchief with her grandfather's loaf of bread flew from her hands.

Swift as hawks after a field mouse the two Brinkerhoff boys swooped down and snatched up her blue bundle.

"Try and get it! Try and get it!" Aaron called out. He held it out to her with an impudent grin on his face. When his brother Arnie grabbed for the bundle, Aaron snatched it away and ran. They played with it as if it were a ball, tossing it back and forth and daring her to chase them.

Ellen stood frozen with fear. What if the bread was torn apart. And the snuffbox fell out. And the British officers learned that Grandfather was a spy! It was too horrible to think of. Grandfather hanging on a gallows tree.

Her hands became fists as she thought how two laughing boys could put them all in such danger.

"Thieves!" she could hear herself shouting. "Stop

those thieves!" She surprised herself by shouting those words in a loud strong voice. She surprised herself, too, by racing after the boys, dodging in and out of the crowds, tripping over children and ducking under the noses of dray horses.

"Stop those thieves!" she screamed. "They stole my bread!"

She ran up to two redcoats who stood on the steps of a bakeshop, eating hot little pies while they flirted with a group of kitchen maids.

"Please, sirs!" she gasped, "those thieves have stolen my bread!"

The soldiers shrugged and laughed. "Plenty of bread inside. The baker has just opened his ovens."

Now the boys were playing a game in front of a tailor's shop. They were tossing the blue bundle across his sign and hurling it between the wooden blades of a giant pair of scissors. Around them a crowd formed a circle to watch the fun.

"Give me my bread!" Ellen shouted as she leaped from one side to the other. She felt as nimble as a lamb without her long skirts and petticoats, but she never was quick enough to catch the bread.

Aaron mocked her. "Give the poor child his bread. He's starving!"

"Starving! Starving!" shrieked little Arnie. He held the bread out to her and then snatched it away when she jumped for it.

Two beggars watched with hungry eyes. Their bony fingers reached out to grab the bread. Even the public pig who ate scraps of garbage in the streets raced around them with greedy alert little eyes. The crowd laughed, but no one helped.

A little old woman who swept the steps of the tailor's shop with a broom of corn straw called out sharply. "What ails you Brinkerhoff boys? Always making trouble! Give the boy his loaf of bread!" She stepped down into the street and shook her broom at them. "Can't you see he's thin and hungry?"

Angrily she pushed her way through the crowd. Her back was so bent she was hardly as tall as Ellen, but she seemed to know what to do.

"Here," she said as she thrust her broom handle into Ellen's hands. "Here, trip them up. Bread is precious these days."

Ellen snatched the broomstick from the old woman. Without a moment's hesitation she raised it up and brought it down with a whack across Aaron's legs. Her eyes were blazing as she watched him duck out of her way. It made her feel good to hear him yell,

"Stop," and see him dance away from her.

Arnie snatched the bundle from his brother's hands, and whirling it about his head, he grinned at her. "Try and get it!" he shrieked as he turned to push his way through the circle of people.

Ellen rushed after Arnie and whacked his legs, too. Her anger was so great she whacked at his legs until he fell sprawling on the ground.

Quick as a flash she scooped up the bundle, dropped her broom and looked for a way out of the circle.

"This way!" cried the little old woman gleefully. She held out her arms and made an opening for Ellen to get through. "Run like the wind, boy," she cried. "They'll be after you."

Ellen raced down the street. Her feet seemed to have wings. "Where to go? Where to hide?" she thought desperately as she looked over her shoulder and saw that the boys and the hungry beggars and even that awful public pig were after her.

Two boys might catch a girl who never had run on cobblestones before. But no one could catch a girl who held her grandfather's secret snuffbox in her arms.

"Stop him!" she could hear Arnie Brinkerhoff shout. "Stop the thief!"

The thief! Why, it was her loaf of bread. And why

would they want it? It was just a game to them. No more important than a snowball.

She jumped over the low stone wall of a church-yard and raced across the flat gravestones. Looking back, she could see that she must have lost the beggars and the pig. Only the boys were following her. And a church warden who ran after her flapping his arms and shouting, "Be gone! Be gone!"

Over the wall she scrambled and into a street filled with haycarts going to the officers' stables. Under one cart and around another she darted. Farmers shook their pitchforks at her as she whirled past. "Don't alarm the horses!" they cried. But Ellen didn't hear them.

She had no idea where she was now as she raced around corners and down streets filled with rubble. Everywhere there were black walls of houses with roofs that had fallen in.

Gasping for breath she darted through a doorway of a broken-down house and crept into an old fire-place to hide. She was sure she had outrun the boys, but she couldn't stop the shaking of her knees. They jerked up and down like puppets on strings.

She sat down in the old ashes of the fireplace, tucked her arms around her knees and put her head on her arms. Her breath came in great sobs and blew the ashes up around her, covering her breeches with a fine dust.

"This must be the way rabbits feel—when the hounds chase them. If only I were back at home— I could crawl into bed and pull the covers over my head."

Those boys! Those horrible boys! To spoil everything at the beginning. It wasn't to have been such a long walk to Front Street. She had done it before with Grandfather.

"And now I don't know where I am," she wailed.

Grandfather had never brought her to the west side of town where the great fire burned block after block last September. It made him too sad to look at it, he said. Six hundred houses had been burned. And Trinity Church. It was lucky the whole city didn't burn up!

Slowly she began to collect her wits. Grandfather would have to find someone else to carry his message. She'd go home and tell him he had asked too much of her. She couldn't go out on the streets and roister about like a boy. She couldn't go sailing across the Bay to a place where she had never been and find a man she had never seen. That was asking too much of a ten-year-old girl. She'd go home and tell him he must find someone else.

She waited a long time to make sure the boys had not followed her. As she waited she grew calm and a strange happy feeling came over her.

She, Ellen Toliver, had fought two boys in front of a crowd of people. She not only had raced them and beaten them but she had saved her grandfather's message. The bread was here with the snuffbox still inside. She could hardly believe it.

As she sat quietly, a new feeling of confidence came to her. "Perhaps I can try to walk to the docks after all." She took a deep breath. "Perhaps I can go to Jersey after all. Grandfather said it wasn't hard. I can start over again from here, if I can find my way to Front Street."

Very carefully she crept out of the fireplace and looked around. There were tents where people must be living amidst the broken-down walls. But she saw no one around. Only stray cats that slunk away in the rubble.

"It must be getting near ten o'clock," she said to herself. There were no church bells to ring the hour, for the wardens had hidden the bells when the British came. She looked up at the hazy sun that struggled wanly in a gray sky. Grandfather always pointed out directions by the shadows the sun cast. "If the sun is on my left side—that must be the east. And the East River would be that way."

Very carefully she picked her way through the black rubble flecked with white snow. And at last she came to streets lined with fine houses and beech and sycamore trees. These streets looked familiar and the breeze had the salty fish smell of the river.

As she stepped quickly along she had a feeling the trip wouldn't be so bad after all.

Six

Long before she reached Front Street she heard the beat of army drums and the shrill piping of the fifes. Trim lines of redcoats marched up and down the streets and formed in squads and companies on all the wharves.

The East River bristled with the masts of small sloops and riverboats, while overhead white gulls circled with loud cries. But nowhere could Ellen see the fat broad-beamed boats of the farmers or the oystermen from Jersey.

Near the Market-house she stopped a spindly little man pushing a wheelbarrow with only two small pumpkins in it.

"Where are the oystermen's boats," she asked anxiously, "or the farmers' boats from Elizabethtown?"

"Oh," he said, "not many of them came over today. Food is scarce and the oyster catch was poor. Those who came started back a few moments ago."

"Back!" cried Ellen. "Why, they can't have gone yet. It's too early for them to leave."

"Well, they have!" he said. "Only British boats here now."

"You must be mistaken," Ellen said. "They must be at another dock." She'd have to hurry to find them.

"Look for yourself, boy," the man called after her. "They say twenty boats are taking troops over to Elizabeth today."

With her heart pounding wildly Ellen ran from one dock to another all up and down Front Street. She raced among the chests and barrels and great coils of rope as she looked at every boat tied up there. She darted among the soldiers and the seamen, but no one stopped her or noticed her.

The man was right. There were only British boats

filling up with soldiers, all along the waterfront. The men sat on planks and were crowded together as closely as kernels of corn on a cob.

"What can I do now?" she thought desperately. "There isn't even a fisherman or an oysterman to ask for a ride." She jingled the coins in her pocket. "If I dared to ask."

It was plain to see that nothing could be done. She felt as gloomy as the dark water lapping at the end of the dock where she stood. "Those redcoats! They think they own the whole world!" She'd tell Grandfather what rough men they were—with hard faces and loud voices. They pushed and shoved and cursed as they climbed on board the sloops. She'd tell Grandfather the docks had not been like this when she came here with him on Sunday afternoon. Surely he would understand there was nothing she could do.

But he'd never understand why she was late when she had started out at nine o'clock. "I can't go home and tell him I dropped the bread," she cried. "He told me to hang on to it. He'll never forgive me for letting those boys grab it away from me."

Perhaps she could get to Elizabeth-town on one of the redcoats' boats. It was probably dangerous, but it would be better than going home to face Grandfather's disappointment. Perhaps, since no one seemed to notice her now, she could slip on board quietly and hide herself under a seat. No one would find her there.

"You could do it," she said to herself. "You could make yourself do it." As she stood there staring at the boats, trying to get up enough courage to start, she was surprised to see one of the redcoats lean across the side of the boat and grin at her.

He was a husky man with a dirty fringe of scraggly hair beneath his black hat. She couldn't take her eyes from his large nose. It was as big and red as a sweet potato.

"What you huggin' so tight?" he asked her. "It smells right good." His fat cheeks shook when he spoke, but his nose looked as if it were anchored fast.

"Oh, don't pester the boy, Dow," said the sad-faced soldier who sat slumped over beside him. His mouth drooped at the corners and looked as tired and woebegone as his eyes. Then he leaned across Dow and said, "I've got a boy back home in London who looks like you. What's your name?"

"Ellen Toliver, sir," she answered.

"How's that?"

Ellen gasped. She had forgotten how she was dressed, but with all the noise he apparently had not heard her. Raising her voice she said, "I said my name is Toliver, sir."

"My boy's name is Tom. But he looks like you. Same pale face. Same big eyes. It makes me homesick to see a boy who favors Tom," he said forlornly.

Ellen could see by his sad face that he really was homesick. But he also looked kind. Perhaps she dared ask him if she could just ride across the Bay with them.

But these were British soldiers. How could she trust an enemy?

Before she could decide what to do, she felt a tug at her blue bundle. "Smells like fresh bread there," she heard the big man say. Quickly Ellen snatched the bundle away. Then suddenly she, herself, was seized around the waist by two big red hands and whisked across the side of the boat. She was too surprised and frozen with fear to make a sound.

The man with the red cheeks and the sweet potato nose laughed as he squashed her down on the bench beside him and clapped a big hand over her mouth. It smelled of fish and salty biscuits and almost smothered her. "No noise from you," he muttered. The shoulders of the two redcoats closed the space above her head.

What was happening to her? This wasn't what she

had meant to do. She felt as if a hummingbird were caught inside her chest, her heart was beating so fast. She stared at the wet brown planks of the deck and the row of black boots and white leggings that stretched to the other side of the boat.

The man bent down and grinned at her. Under his bushy eyebrows his blue eyes were laughing at her. "Surprised, be ye?" he asked.

Ellen could hear the homesick soldier on her other side say impatiently, "What you doing that for, Dow?"

"Because I'm hungry as a bear in spring. That's why. Nothing but salt biscuits and dried herring, day after day."

Hungry! Ellen gasped at the thought of it. She kicked her legs and pushed her elbows and tried to pull her mouth free.

It was too late to get back to the dock. She could tell the sloop was casting off, for she could hear the sails being hoisted, and flapping loudly in the breeze, then smoothing out as the boat came about in the river and turned into the wind. She felt it rock as it headed into the waves.

The man took his hand away from her mouth. "No squawking!" he warned her. "You can sit up now."

As she sat up cautiously and looked around, the

thin man with the sad face peered at her sharply. "Are you all right, boy?" he asked with concern. "My friend is a joker."

"A joker!" snorted the other. "I'm hungry." Then he turned to Ellen. "Dow's my name. And this here is Higgins—him who's homesick for his boy in London. And you're Toliver, you say."

Ellen nodded her head. She craned her neck to look at the ships in the harbor. They were sailing past seven great warships anchored there—the seven British warships that she and Grandfather had seen from the Battery. He said the British had brought seven hundred ships all told, last summer. And thirty thousand soldiers who had camped on Staten Island. Thirty thousand soldiers! That was almost twice as many men as there were people in New York.

"Are we going to Elizabeth-town?" she asked the homesick Mr. Higgins.

He shrugged. "That's what our orders are," he said. "You are the picture of my boy Tom, I swear."

Dow smiled at her as he took a knife from his belt and pulled it from its case. "Now that we are friends" —he coughed politely—"now that we are friends, I'll just share your fresh bread with us."

He leaned down and quickly snatched Ellen's blue

bundle from her mittened hands.

"Oh, sir!" she cried as she clung to the blue kerchief, "I can't share it. It's for an old man's birthday present!"

His thick red tongue ran around his lips. "I could smell that good fresh bread when you stood there on the dock," said Dow as he slapped her hands away. "I said to myself, 'That boy will be happy to share his bread with a soldier of the King.' "

"But it's for my grandfather's friend!" cried Ellen. "Please give it back to me."

"Too bad for your grandfather's friend," Dow grunted as he fumbled awkwardly with the knot in the kerchief.

Ellen stared at his knife. The bright gleaming blade in Dow's rough hands seemed more awful than a sword at her throat. In a moment he would cut into the bread and find the snuffbox. Then he'd open the snuffbox and find Grandfather's message to General Washington. Soon he'd know that she was a spy's messenger. Grandfather had told her to say she didn't know anything about it. But they'd find out where she lived and who she belonged to and Grandfather would be caught! She knew well enough what would happen then.

Suddenly, without thinking what she did, she

snatched the blue bundle from Dow's hands so quickly he lost his grip. In an instant she tucked it under her jacket, doubled up, and locked her arms beneath her legs.

The sad-faced Higgins laughed so hard his tall black hat almost fell from his head. "You're a quick one, Toliver."

Dow's fat jowls shook with anger. "Why you little rascal," he snarled as he tried to pry her arms loose. "Give me back that bread!"

"No!" said Ellen stubbornly. Her arms were locked in fear so tightly she could not have moved them if she'd tried.

"Give me that bread!" Dow grunted as he pulled at her pigtail.

"No," said Ellen. She winced from the pain at the back of her head.

"I haven't had fresh bread for weeks," Dow complained, tugging at her arm with his fat red hands. "And so I mean to have it!" He pulled harder on her arm.

Ellen's arms felt like an iron clamp. "You won't have my bread. I won't give it to you," she muttered. And then she remembered the corncakes her mother had given her. "There are some good corncakes in my

pocket, sir. Take both of them."

The redcoats sitting on the bench in front of them turned around and started to laugh at the sight of a small boy defying big old Dow.

"Hang on, boy!" they shouted.

Ellen hung on. "Take the corncakes, sir. They are just as good. Right in my pocket beside you."

She could hear Higgins laughing until he began to hiccup and gasp for air. "He's like an oyster shell!" Higgins could hardly catch his breath. "You'll have to pry him open."

From the stern of the boat a voice roared at them. "Stop that ruckus amidship! You'll send us all into the waves!"

The men became quiet at once. In the silence Ellen heard only the waves banging along the sides of the sloop. And Higgins's muffled hiccups.

She held her breath as she sat doubled up over the bread. If the officer had seen her that would be the end of her. She was grateful the broad shoulders of the men covered her.

At last Dow shrugged and said from the side of his mouth. "You little scamp. I'll take those corncakes."

"They're in my pocket. Take them all. And welcome."

Dow cut a piece of corncake and put it in his mouth on the end of his knife. "That bread is squashed flat by now. So keep it! I hope the old gizzard likes squashed bread."

Higgins nudged her with his sharp elbow. "Not bad, Toliver! You're a spunky little rogue—just like my Tom back home."

Ellen glanced up at Higgins. He seemed to mean what he said. No one had ever called her spunky. She eased the blue bundle up under her jacket, and kept her arms tightly locked across the bulge as she cautiously sat up.

Seven

Grandfather had said that the trip across the Bay to Elizabeth-town would take about two hours of good sailing. But with a cold blustery wind in her face it seemed longer to Ellen. As the sloop plowed through the rough green waters she watched the chunks of floating ice that had come down from the north. She shivered as she heard the boat crunch through them. High above the white sails she could see that the sun had come out among ragged patches of clouds. But it had no warmth.

The tall mast made her think of the gallows. She had walked past the gallows in New York, holding fast to her grandfather's hand as she stared at it. Thieves and murderers were hanged there—and spies also, she now knew.

Ezra had gone to a hanging once. Her father had been so angry he whipped him for it—just for looking. No son of his could gape at a hanging, father had said. Only grown-ups could do that, Ellen thought. And now his daughter might be part of a hanging— if the officer found she was a spy.

Her imagination ran wild and shivers went down her back. Of course, she could pretend to be surprised when they found the snuffbox. But they'd still find out about Grandfather, and they'd hang him as a spy. The British officers would take over his house. And what would she and her mother do then?

At the thought of it, tears came to Ellen's eyes. Higgins must have been watching her because he said, "What's a big boy like you crying about?"

"I'm not crying," Ellen muttered. "It's the cold wind in my eyes."

He patted her arm. "I'm right sorry we got you on this boat," he said. "But you'll get yourself home all right. All you Yankees are plucky."

"Plucky!" scoffed Dow. "Just plain fools. Foolish enough to fight the King. And in winter yet," he growled. "Back home no army fights in winter!" He put up his hands and rubbed his red ears.

"Zounds!" cried Higgins. "This war will be over in no time." A smile spread over his gloomy face. "And we'll be going home! Why, it's bound to be over soon. They can't hold out much longer. We took three thousand prisoners when we took Fort Washington up there on Hudson's River."

"And a hundred and fifty cannon," Dow reminded him, "when we took Fort Lee on the Jersey side. Sent them running like rabbits over to Pennsylvania! Rag-tag army!" Dow laughed. "Some have hunting jackets with fringe—like Indians. Some have farmers' smocks —any old thing—all marching together. I been soldiering all over Europe and I never saw an army look like that."

"They're sharpshooters, though," Higgins said seriously.

"You know what!" said Dow. "They got only a band of cloth on the sleeve to show what regiment they're in." He guffawed and slapped his knee.

"They can shoot, though," Higgins said again, gloomily.

"Oh, they can shoot all right," said Dow, "when they ain't running away. Like at Kip's Bay."

Ellen remembered hearing talk about Kip's Bay. The Patriot soldiers had turned tail and run away. No one could believe it.

Dow gave her a nudge. "We never saw nothing but their backs. They are all a bunch of cowards!"

"No!" Ellen protested. "They are not cowards!"

Dow peered at her. "You know what! You're mighty pretty for a boy. Almost as pretty as a girl."

"I am not!" Ellen ducked her head to hide her alarm. "But they are not cowards!" she said stubbornly.

Inwardly she gasped in horror. She had said too much.

"Oh, ho! A rebel we have!" said Dow as he looked at her from under his heavy eyebrows. "A hot little rebel boy."

A burly soldier with a scar across his forehead turned around and snorted. "Throw the rebel overboard. There'll be one less rebel to fight."

Ellen tightened her arms around the bundle inside her jacket and ducked her head to make herself as small as possible. She felt as cold as an icicle and yet her face was damp with sweat. If they threw her overboard she'd take the loaf of bread down with her.

They'd never, never get the snuffbox away from her.

Higgins threw back his head and started to sing in a loud twangy voice, "Come all you soldiers bold, lend an ear, lend an ear." Immediately the men around him sang out a loud refrain, "Lend an ear, lend an ear."

Higgins sang the next line, "Come all you soldiers bold, lend an ear—" And the men boomed back the refrain, "Lend an ear, lend an ear."

Higgins sang verse after verse and the men joined in the refrain. Ellen was glad because it took their minds off her. By the time they had sung "Hearts of Oak" and "Old King Cole," she felt more relaxed.

"They must have been teasing me," she thought to herself. "They wouldn't really throw me overboard. Higgins wouldn't let them." Feeling relieved, she began to smile to herself. She had spoken right up to those rough soldiers in their red coats and their big black hats. And with a secret message right under their noses. After all those weeks of bowing her head and curtsying politely to the redcoats at home, she had spoken up and said what she thought. As the men sang "The British Grenadiers," Ellen began humming along too, very softly.

At length they came to the narrow channel where the tide carried them swiftly along. With sails set wide, like the wings of a white bird, the boat was skimming now instead of straining through the waves. Neither Dow nor Higgins noticed when she sat up straight and looked around. She watched the parade of boats as they filed down the channel. White sails ahead of them and white sails behind them. Twenty boats, the man on Front Street had told her. And all of them filled with soldiers.

On either side of them the shores were close enough to see. To the left were snowy fields and orchards and little brown farmhouses. That must be Staten Island. She remembered the map in her father's schoolhouse.

Once, Ezra had explained the map of Long Island and New York Bay and all the colonies along the shore. Her father had shrugged his shoulders and said that a little girl didn't need to know things like that —unless she was going to be a peddler. And he certainly didn't mean to have a peddler for a daughter.

"He didn't know he'd have a spy for a daughter," Ellen said to herself.

She was glad that her brother had explained the map to her, for it was easy to guess that this swampy land on the right, with all the pine trees, would be New Jersey. And the end of her journey! Soon she'd be jumping off the boat and racing for the Jolly Fox

Tavern. She'd be safe inside with her grandfather's friends. At the thought of it she could feel the load of worry rise up from her shoulders and float away. She felt so happy and relieved she started humming to herself.

"What's amiss with you?" Dow growled at her.

Ellen shrank back. She didn't want any trouble with Dow.

"You scare the boy," Higgins spoke up sharply. "He didn't ask to come along, did he?"

"What's he afraid of?" Dow asked. "Me? Are you afraid of me, boy?"

"No," said Ellen quickly. It wasn't true. She really was scared of him, and she wished he would leave her alone. But Dow kept staring at her, and she had to drop her eyes. "Well, maybe—a little," she confessed.

"A big chap like you shouldn't be afraid of anything," sneered Dow.

"Talk right back to him, Toliver." Higgins's face was red and his black stubble of beard looked dark across his chin.

"I can't," said Ellen without looking up.

"Why"—Dow made his eyes look round and innocent—"I'm as gentle as a morn in May."

Higgins snorted. For a long time he sat staring off at the clouds in the sky. At last he said to Ellen, "When I was a boy I had a brother who pestered me like that. I had to learn to talk back to him. Funny thing was—when he saw I wasn't afraid of him, he didn't bother me any more." He turned and smiled. "Bullies are like that."

Ellen remembered Dicey and the way she had bawled when the Brinkerhoff boys washed her face with snow. Dicey's boldness seemed to collapse all at once like one of those balloons made of a pig's bladder when the air is let out.

After a long silence she said, "Are you ever afraid of anything now, Mr. Higgins?"

Dow overheard her and laughed loudly. "I'm never afraid of anything," he boasted.

The soldier with the scar across his forehead turned around again and hooted. "Never? What about White Plains?"

Dow's face flushed red with anger. "Never!" he snapped.

"Yah! Yah!" shouted the other redcoats around him.

Higgins did not answer her question right away. At last he leaned down and said in a low voice that only she could hear, "Well, son, I'll answer you true as I would answer my own son back home. Sometimes."

He nodded his head. "Sometimes I am afraid—as many men are. Being afraid is nothing to be ashamed of." He threw a sidelong glance at her. "But when something has to be done," he said firmly, "don't wonder and wonder about being afraid. If it's important to you—do the best you can."

Ellen stared up at the white sails. This trip was important. At first it had been important to her because it was very important to Grandfather. But now she had seen the British soldiers with their guns and bayonets—hundreds of them—going to fight the Patriots' army. Now she was eager to help General Washington. Now she was glad to be part of the chain of people who wanted the Patriots to win, and would get information to him. Important information, her grandfather had said. She was impatient to get to the Jolly Fox Tavern and deliver the loaf of bread.

At last she could see on the right the church spires and the frosty roofs of a town white against the pine trees. Some of the houses and taverns were built on the street that ran along the waterfront and some on top of the bluff behind them. Everywhere the lines of marching men looked like busy ants on an anthill. As the boat came closer she strained her eyes to see a sign of the Jolly Fox Tavern.

"I hope the Shannons have a crackling fire and a hot meat pie," Ellen thought.

With sails flapping noisily, their boat headed toward a dock and glided in for a landing. Ropes were tossed to the dockhands who waited to pull them in.

"All ashore!" shouted the officer in the stern. "And step smartly."

The men stood up and stretched. Ellen was glad the officer could not see her. She quickly scrambled up on the dock and when she was well out of Dow's reach she turned and grinned at him. "Goodbye, Mr. Dow!" she cried happily.

"Hold your tongue," growled Dow.

"Goodbye, Mr. Higgins," she called to him. "I'll remember the things you told me."

"I'll remember you, Toliver."

Ellen's brown eyes were sparkling and her cheeks were red as winter apples. She slipped the blue bundle out of her jacket and swung it jauntily around her head as she turned to run.

Dow grunted. "Pert little beggar," he said to Higgins. "Too pretty for a boy, to my mind."

But Ellen didn't hear that. She was racing to the Jolly Fox Tavern.

Eight

$\mathcal{E}$llen was so happy she felt like shouting, "Here I am! Here I am at last!" And she could have shouted too, and not have been heard at all—with all the noise in the little town. The cries of cannoneers, the rumbling of wagon trains, the pounding of the heavy boots of marching men filled the air of Elizabeth-town. And over it all sounded the drums, the screeching fifes and the wailing bagpipes.

She skipped down the street that ran beside the waterfront. One dock after another was filled with soldiers climbing from the boats and hoisting up their knapsacks.

She looked eagerly at all the signs hanging above the shops and taverns that stood against the bluff on the opposite side of the street. Nowhere could she see a sign for the Jolly Fox Tavern. Ellen was puzzled. Grandfather said it would be here and not hard to find, for Elizabeth was a small town.

She began to feel anxious and decided to ask someone. Carrying her blue bundle behind her, she walked up to a big ruddy-faced workman who had stopped his oxen by a dock and was loading his oxcart with wooden army chests. His huge muscles almost burst the sleeves of his woolen shirt. Across his fat stomach was stretched a well-worn leather apron.

"Where is Mr. Shannon's tavern?" Ellen shouted above the noise of the drums and the bagpipes.

"Must be here somewhere." The man's voice was as deep and rumbling as a foghorn.

"It's at the sign of the Jolly Fox," Ellen shouted.

"Jolly Fox Tavern?" The man wiped his hands on his shirt sleeves. "Never saw it here in Amboy."

"Amboy!" cried Ellen. "Isn't this Elizabeth-town?"

"Nay. It's Perth Amboy." The man jumped up on his cart and started to push and pull at the army chests to pile them up.

Ellen stared at him—speechless. Higgins had said their boat was coming to Elizabeth-town.

"Elizabeth is back there." The man pointed with his chin. "Back along the shore—about ten miles or so."

"But how can I get to Elizabeth?" Ellen cried in a high frightened voice.

"Swim—maybe," he laughed. "But walk—likely."

In her alarm, Ellen felt as if her head were about to spin off her shoulders. She couldn't think and she suddenly felt very hot. She must be in a nightmare. Grandfather had said there was only one thing to do when she got off the boat. Walk to the tavern of friendly Mr. Shannon. He hadn't said she might have to walk ten miles! In the winter! When it was getting late and without knowing the way!

When the man looked at her frightened face he climbed down from his cart and bent over her so she could hear him clearly. "Stagecoaches go to Elizabeth," he said. "If you have money to pay."

Of course she had money to pay. She had the coins in her pocket.

"See the big inn yonder," he said kindly as he pointed down the street. "See the fenced-in yard beside it. The stagecoach comes by there to pick up passengers."

"Oh, thank you," said Ellen gratefully.

In all her life she never had been on a stagecoach, but she had seen them rolling along the streets in New York. She would climb up and get a seat on top beside the driver and she would ask him to stop in front of the Jolly Fox Tavern so she'd have no more searching to do.

As she picked her way through the crowds that filled the street, she was surprised to see so many men who looked different from the familiar redcoats. Some had short plaid skirts and bare knees and they marched to the tune of bagpipes. Grandfather had told her they were British subjects who came from Scotland. Highlanders, he called them. But she stared in surprise at the other big men with hard faces under great heavy hats who spoke in words she couldn't understand at all. They couldn't be British soldiers, for some wore blue coats and others green.

"And yet," Ellen said to herself, "they have guns with bayonets and they carry knapsacks—so they must be fighting men."

Carefully she edged her way past them looking up at their grim faces and clutching her bundle tightly in her arms. She hoped none of them would notice her.

"Why," she thought suddenly, "they must be the Hessians." She had heard about the terrible Hessians after the battles on Long Island. Everyone at home resented the German soldiers who hired themselves to King George to fight his wars for him. They had come over here to kill colonists for money. She ducked her head and darted past them.

When she reached the inn, Ellen was dismayed to see that in order to get to the front door she would have to cross a yard filled with the restless horses of the Hessian officers and the grooms who took care of them. She stood at the fence and tried to summon enough courage to walk to the door to ask when the next stagecoach would leave for Elizabeth-town. But nothing in the world would induce her to go inside where the Hessians were.

Since there was no sign of a stagecoach in the yard, nor anyone there she could ask, Ellen slipped quietly along the street beside the inn where she spoke to the only person around who wasn't a soldier. He was an old man who was unloading firewood from a cart near the small taproom door of the inn. His boots were bundles of straw, tied round his legs with ropes, and his hat had once been an animal of some kind, but it was hard to tell what sort now. The tail, which must have been bushy at one time, was worn to a scraggly rope.

"Can you tell me where the stagecoach starts?" she asked.

The old man turned around. He looked thin and tired and his face was so gnarled it seemed to be made from a dried apple. Little bunches of gray hairs grew from his ears. He sucked in his wrinkled lips and squinted at her with sharp beady eyes.

"If you wait for a stagecoach," he said sourly, "you'll wait till Doomsday!"

"Why?" Ellen asked anxiously.

The man slammed four logs down on the ground before he spoke.

"Because there ain't none!"

"None at all?" Ellen cried.

"The British took them. Only officers ride in the stage now. No common people." The man angrily yanked more chunks of wood from his cart and swore at his old horse.

"But how can I get to Elizabeth-town?"

"Can't." The old man spat a long brown stream of tobacco juice against the tree trunk, loaded the firewood on his shoulder and shuffled on bowed legs to the taproom door. It slammed behind him.

Ellen's heart fell to the soles of her feet. Her legs would no longer hold her up and she sank down on a bench under the gnarled old tree beside the door. She sat so stiff and straight she seemed to be carved from a piece of wood—except for her twisting hands. She felt like a fly in a spider's web. She couldn't go on to find the Shannons, and she couldn't go back. There was no way to go home now.

She couldn't even think. If only the noise would stop so she could think. There was so much shouting and playing of fifes and bagpipes it made her head whirl as fast as her mother's spinning wheel.

Why had Grandfather thought she could do this? Why had he sent her off across the Bay to a place she knew nothing about? With no way to get back home again. Why had he thought a ten-year-old girl could do a man's work? She stared at the company of Highlanders marching by in their plaid kilts and their bare knees, but she hardly saw them.

Her thoughts raced around and around like squirrels in a whirling cage. Round and round without stopping.

When the old man came back, Ellen saw that someone had given him a chunk of black bread. He was gnawing it with his gums and gulping it down as if he were starved. He must be very poor to be so hungry.

She jumped to her feet. "Why, I could pay him to take me in his cart!" She was so excited the words tumbled out. "Look! I'll pay you—more—if you'll take me to Elizabeth-town." She snatched the coins from her pocket and held out her hand. "Here! I'll pay you all of them!"

The old man looked greedily at the coins in her outstretched hand. His fingers twitched as he reached for them, but at the last moment he put his hands behind his back and shook his head.

"Nope," he said firmly.

"But why not?" cried Ellen.

"Elizabeth's north. I go west to go home. Hardly get there before dark as it is."

Her hopes fell to her feet like a china cup breaking in a hundred pieces.

"I suppose I could walk," she said forlornly. But she knew she never could do that. Not ten miles— all alone. When she had walked ten miles before, she and Mother had kept each other company and given each other strength.

"Can't walk on that road!" cried the man. "That's a right busy road—out past the soldiers' camp. Lots of redcoats on horses. They'd run you down!" Ellen

remembered the officers on horses in New York. She was sure they'd run down anyone who got in their way.

"Perhaps," she said stubbornly, "some woodcutter who goes north would give me a ride—"

"Small chance of that," the man snorted angrily. "Nobody picks up strangers in these times." He spat at the tree and wiped his mouth with a thin claw of a hand. "Too risky to pick up strangers who might rob you—or even kill you. Don't you know there is a war on, boy?"

"Yes, I know, but—" Ellen began.

"People around here used to be friendly. But no more." He stopped his work and squinted at her. "You're a runaway, ain't you?" he said as he leaned over to look at her more closely. "Better go back home, boy. No good running away now. Things are bad everywhere."

"I'm *not* running away from home!" Ellen was so angry her brown eyes flashed and her words came out like hot sparks. "My home isn't here! And I must go to Elizabeth-town. Can't you understand me?"

The man stared at her in surprise and bewilderment. Then he shrugged and said. "Well, can't be done. Not in these days." He turned his back and bit off a huge piece of bread. All Ellen could see was the scrawny tail that hung from his cap.

"Toliver!" she heard someone call out. "Hey, Toliver!"

It was Higgins. The men from the boat were marching past the inn with their muskets on their shoulders. They seemed like old friends in this town full of strangers. "How you faring, Toliver?" Higgins cried out eagerly.

Dow was marching by also. "Toliver!" she heard him shout. "Hope the old gizzard likes squashed bread." He gave her a big grin and marched on laughing.

"Why," thought Ellen, "Dow thinks this queer old man is the friend who had the birthday. This funny old man, with his toothless mouth so full he could hardly chew!"

Ellen started to laugh. Clutching the bread beneath her jacket, she ran to catch up with Higgins and march along beside him.

"You're a mighty cheerful little scamp," he said as he smiled down at her.

"I'm so happy to see you, Mr. Higgins," she said laughing. She thought to herself, "Higgins is my good friend—even if he is one of the enemy." She felt funny thinking it, but it comforted her to have a friend in this strange and frightening place.

"There are soldiers here wearing short skirts!" She could hardly stop laughing when she thought of them. "Their knees are bare and their legs are hairy. I should think they'd be cold when the wind blows."

Higgins laughed to see her so merry.

"And there are Hessians too!" Ellen shuddered. "I know they are Hessians. They look so fierce they scare me."

Suddenly she could feel tears splashing down on her jacket and all her efforts to be brave broke down. She was laughing and crying at the same time. Laughing and crying both together. What had happened to her?

Higgins's kind dark eyes were filled with concern as he looked at her. "What's amiss with you, Toliver?"

Ellen took a deep breath before she blurted out, "I wanted to go to Elizabeth-town and the boat brought me to Amboy instead."

"So this is Amboy!" said Higgins, surprised. "How far away is Elizabeth-town?" he asked.

"Ten miles!"

"Whew!" Higgins glanced up at the sun. "Must be three o'clock. That's quite a march," he said. "But if you hurry you'll make it all right."

Ellen was running to keep up with him. "But I'm afraid of going by myself."

"Being afraid is nothing to hold you back," said Higgins. "Just square your shoulders and start. Things aren't so bad after you start."

He was fumbling in his pocket. "Hold out your hand, Toliver," he said, and he pressed a coin into her mitten. "There. Go get on the stagecoach and you'll be there long before dark."

Before she could tell him that she already had money in her pocket and there was no stagecoach, an officer on a big gray horse dashed up to her. "Be gone, boy!" he cried angrily as he flicked at her with his riding crop. "I'll have no boys begging from my men!" the officer roared at her.

Ellen ducked, but the horse kept edging her over to the side of the road and turned so she couldn't dodge around him. She couldn't even see Higgins as he marched away.

Very carefully she opened her hand to look at the coin—a fat silver coin—bigger than she had ever seen. And she couldn't even thank him for it. She might never see Higgins again, but she'd never forget him.

He had given her something more important than

money. He had been her friend. Now she knew she could do it somehow.

Back to the old woodcutter she ran to ask the way to Elizabeth-town. "I'm going to walk!" she said to the old man. "I'm going to walk to Elizabeth-town!" she said again when he did not seem to understand her.

He looked at her with a faint smile on his face. "Well," he said as he gulped down the last of the bread, "I did it myself many a time when I was young and had young legs—like yours." He took off his cap and scratched his head as he squinted at the sun. "Must be nigh on to three o'clock. But it's a good road. You can walk it at night."

"At night!" cried Ellen. "I'm going to run most of the way to get there before dark. I've walked ten miles before," she said to the old man. "I can do it again when there is naught else to be done."

She sounded bold. She sounded like a person who could run ten miles and never stop for breath. But inside she was trembling.

"Well, start running then," the old man said, and he turned back to his firewood.

Nine

Running was easy enough at first. Swinging her blue bundle at her side, Ellen followed a company of soldiers stepping along in double time to the fast beating of the drums. And after the men had come to the end of the town and turned into the fields to their campgrounds, she trotted behind the wagon trains. She could see that the wagons were piled high with things for the soldiers' camp—chests and canvas tents and great iron pots for cooking.

On either side of the road, soldiers were setting up

tents and building shacks. There was a bright red glow of campfires back in the fields as far as she could see. A pale blue haze of smoke drifted over the fields.

"It frightens me to see so many men getting ready to fight our army." The thought of the message in her loaf of bread made her run all the more quickly. It kept her from thinking about how hungry she was now, and how the cold wind at her back cut through her wool jacket.

But after she had passed the noisy hubbub in the fields around the camp, Ellen slowed down, for the road was rough and there were no drums beating a quick march to help her hurry. "If I can't run all the way to Elizabeth," she panted, "at least I can keep up a fast walk. I'll get there before dark."

Except for a group of horsemen who dashed past her there was no one on the road that wound through the snowy countryside. "There is something queer about this road," she thought to herself. "It looks like the roads back home, but it's different."

As far as she could tell there were the same snowy fields and fences made of the gnarled roots of trees. The same brown houses close to the road, the same orchards with a few dried apples clinging to bare branches.

But there were no people anywhere. There were no cows in the barns, no sheep in the sheepfolds, nor even chickens pecking in the farmyards. It was like walking in a strange, silent dream.

"There must be people inside," she thought, for in spite of the tightly closed windows, she could see thin wisps of smoke drifting up from the chimneys and blowing away in the wind.

What a strange place. Not like Long Island. The people there had been friendly—when she and Mother walked the ten miles to New York in November. Sometimes they had been asked inside to warm themselves by the fire.

New Jersey was different. There was nothing to do now but just keep marching along by herself. She remembered a song her father used to sing when he'd come home after drilling with the village militia. "Blow the trumpets, 'To Arms.'" That was all she could remember at first. "From the east to the west blow the trumpets, 'To Arms!'" Father had told her Tom Paine wrote it and called it "The Liberty Tree."

"Let the far and the near—all unite with a cheer—in defense of our Liberty Tree." Father's eyes really sparkled when he sang that song. She liked to remember him that way.

"Let the far and the near," she chanted a rhythm for her marching feet.

"Let the far and the near—all unite with a cheer— in defense of our Liberty Tree. Let the far and the near —all unite with a cheer—" Her voice grew strong as she sang it over and over. "—in defense of our Liberty Tree."

Keeping time to her song, Ellen rounded a bend, and stopped short at what she saw. The road disappeared in a woods. She had seen the woods ahead, but she hadn't thought that the road would go right through the middle of it.

Since the winter branches were bare, she could look deep into the forest of brown tree trunks and evergreens. Trees beyond trees as far as she could see. They seemed to go on for miles. The lonely road curved around a huge pine tree and disappeared. Everywhere there were sure to be unknown dangers. Prowling animals! Bears! Thieves! She could go no further.

I can't do it! I can't go on!

But you must do it, Ellen.

I can't! I'm only ten.

A courier is waiting for your message.

I can't! I won't!

●

There is naught else to be done. You must!

Ellen stood and looked at the dark road curving ahead into the silent forest. "Well, when there's something hard to be done," she said at last, "just square your shoulders and start."

Then she pulled her cap over her ears and raced down the road into the woods, looking from side to side as her feet flew over the frozen ground. Behind every tree there seemed to lurk a monster; under every bush, a wild and hungry animal waited to spring out at her.

"If only I can get to the end of the woods," she gasped.

She could almost feel things clawing at her back. But she dared not look over her shoulder to see what they were.

"Run faster, Ellen! Run faster!" she cried as she felt the wind rush past her face.

When at last she had to slow down, gasping for breath, she feared she would be flung to the ground and torn apart.

Nothing happened. There were no monsters behind her. She could see not even one squirrel nor one small rabbit. The woods looked quiet and serene.

Patches of fresh white snow lay on the carpet of

brown leaves. Snow flecked the trunks of the great forest trees and collected in drifts like white pillows on the branches of the evergreens. Red berries that had not been eaten by the birds sparkled on dogwood branches. If there were any animals here, they were asleep in burrows or hollow logs. All around her the woods were peaceful.

"Annabelle would like this." Ellen surprised herself with the thought. The dogwood berries made her think of her cousin. Last winter they had had fun decorating the church for Annabelle's wedding. When they went to the woods to gather greens and red berries, Annabelle had cried out happily, "Why, the forest is more beautiful in winter than it is in summer."

The forest was beautiful, and Ellen was no longer afraid of it. As she trotted along she realized she no longer was fearful at all.

After a while the quiet was broken by the sound of a dog barking and the thudding of a horse's hooves on the hard dirt road. Ellen looked over her shoulder and saw a small dog jumping angrily at the heels of a skinny old horse. Paying no attention to the dog the horse plodded along heavily. The steam from his nose looked like the steam from a kettle on the hearth.

The rider was a man so thin he seemed to be made

of sticks of kindling wrapped in a fluttering coat. His chin rested on a bunch of straw at his throat and a long pointed nose seemed to hold it in place. From each arm hung big woven baskets, limp and empty.

Ellen slipped behind a pine tree. But the little dog had seen her and ran in circles about her feet barking wildly.

"Why you hiding there, boy?" the man called out in a thin high voice with a twang at the edges.

Ellen held her breath.

"Are you a neighbor—or a runaway?" asked the man suspiciously. "You got a gun?"

"I'm not a runaway," said Ellen, "and I haven't any gun."

"Then come out and show yourself."

Slowly Ellen stepped out from behind the tree. She could see now that it was not a bundle of straw at his throat. It was a dirty scraggly beard. More straw-colored hair hung down his back in a bushy clump. "What's that in your hand?" the man seemed to talk through his long nose.

"Only a loaf of bread." Ellen held up the blue bundle for the man to see. The dog barked and jumped for it so wildly she had to hold it high above her head to keep it away from him.

"Where you going?"

"To Elizabeth-town."

"To Elizabeth! Thirteen miles!" He whistled through the space where his two front teeth were missing. "You'll never make it! And besides it will be dark as pitch before you get to Elizabeth."

Ellen stared at him. "Did you say thirteen miles!" she cried. "I thought it was ten! And I've walked two or three miles already."

"It may be ten miles as a crow flies, but it's thirteen miles by road from Amboy. You've walked about two, I'd say. That leaves eleven more to go."

Ellen was too disappointed to say another word. Perhaps the man was wrong.

"Well," he grunted as he wiped his finger across the end of his nose, "my house is only a half mile from Elizabeth. Get up behind me. I need a helper to hold these baskets."

As if he had understood what his master said, the horse turned his head to look at Ellen and snorted disapprovingly through his big loose lips. Ellen jumped back. She had never ridden a horse before.

"Step lively, boy." The man spoke crossly.

The horse rolled his eyes and shook the leathery skin that stretched over his ribs. He looked far from happy at having another rider, Ellen thought. And the man did not look friendly either. But she never could walk eleven more miles. Since there was nothing else she could do, she'd have to take the ride.

The farmer slipped his foot from the stirrup and reached down a bony hand to help her.

"How do I climb up?" Ellen asked.

"Never been on a horse before?" cried the man in surprise. "A big boy like you?"

"No," said Ellen. She was going to say, "My father was a schoolmaster. He didn't have a horse," but she thought better of it.

"Then put your foot here, and I'll give you a hoist."

Ellen put her foot in the stirrup and awkwardly climbed and squirmed her way up behind him, clutching the loaf of bread to her chest with one hand.

She was glad she didn't have skirts and petticoats to get in the way as she straddled the horse's bony back. Very carefully she tucked her blue bundle inside her jacket and arranged the handles of the baskets on her arms. When she leaned forward and put her arms around the man's waist, she knew the bread was safe between her chest and his thin back.

From the odd smell of his baskets, it was hard to guess what he had carried in them. But his bushy hair that tickled her face smelled of sweet wood smoke. It was a comforting smell, although sitting behind him like this was an uncomfortable way to travel. The bouncing made her teeth chatter and jarred her spine. Still, it was better than walking eleven miles with the dog jumping at her and trying to get her bread.

The man pointed a long finger at the little dog. "Go home to your master," he commanded sternly. "Now," he said, when he saw the dog scurry off, "What's your name, boy?"

"Toliver." She could say that name without stumbling now.

"Mine's Murdock."

He handed back some oatcakes that he took from his pocket. "Most boys are hungry," he said.

Hungry! She was starved! She had given her corncakes to Dow on the boat. When he looked over his shoulder and saw that she had gobbled them up quickly, he handed her two more. But he didn't ask her any questions. They rode in silence to the end of the woods and out along the road, passing more closed-up farmhouses. She wanted to ask him about the people inside, but Mr. Murdock was not a talkative man. She could not guess whether he was for the British or for the Patriots.

He said nothing when he had to stop his horse to let some soldiers ride by. Best not to ask him which side he was on—if she wanted to continue her ride. He'd be quite surprised if he knew he was helping the Patriots—especially if he was a Tory.

These were mixed-up times all right.

Ellen remembered Long Island and the long trip that she and her mother had made. No one ever asked the refugees who staggered along the roads which side they were on. All of them were people in trouble. Some of them had great rolls of bedding and cooking pots on their backs, and some pulled carts piled high with household goods. On top of everything rode small children in baskets and the old people. Farm people along the way were kind to them.

She peered around Mr. Murdock's arm and asked, "Why are those houses all closed up so tightly?"

The question seemed to make him angry.

Ellen could feel his back grow stiff and straight as he cried out, "People have to stay behind locked doors these days—since the British came! It's those redcoats! They take everything! Just walk in and take anything they want! Most farmers hide their cows in the woods —and pigs and chickens, too."

At the sound of the horse's hooves splashing through

water Ellen looked down fearfully. They were crossing a stream. It was shallow enough, but thin sheets of ice formed around the rocks at the edge.

Suddenly Mr. Murdock stood up in the stirrups and waved his thin arm as if he had a sword in his hand. "King George ain't going to push us around! We'll fight back!" he cried.

Ellen had tried to keep hold of his waist as he stood up. But as she raised her arms she could feel the blue bundle slip down from under her jacket. She lunged for it.

"My bread!" she shrieked. "Stop the horse!"

"Your what?" cried Mr. Murdock as he threw a startled look over his shoulder. He yanked back on the reins. The horse was startled too. He slipped and slid on the icy rocks, sank down on his haunches and darted up again.

"My bread!" Ellen screamed. "My loaf of bread is gone!"

Mr. Murdock reined in the horse by the side of the stream. "Did you drop my baskets?" he yelled.

Quickly Ellen clutched the saddle with both hands, swung her leg over the horse's rump and slid down his side. She didn't stop to wonder about the slippery rocks or how deep the water might be. She waded into the stream up to her knees until she could scoop up her bundle.

"He might have told me he was going to stand up," she grumbled as she opened the kerchief and looked at the bread. It was soggy, but the good strong crust had held its shape.

Mr. Murdock didn't see the need to apologize. Instead he dismounted, gathered up his baskets and shook the water from them angrily. He glared at her. "Why did you drop my baskets? It was just lucky they weren't filled with the leather hides I took to Amboy."

Ellen hung her head, but she felt defiant. Why, it was his fault, she thought. He should have told her he was going to stand up.

"You made me drop my bread when you stood up," she declared stubbornly. "I had to get it before it floated away and was lost."

"That was a witless thing to do. Happens my wife would give you another loaf."

"This is a present for an old man's birthday. My mother baked it this morning," Ellen said hastily. "But I'm sorry I dropped your baskets."

"Come on then. Climb back up on the horse," he said.

When they were well on their way, Mr. Murdock turned and looked back at her suspiciously. "You're a queer one," he said. "You got something inside that bread?"

Ellen gasped. She buried her face in his back and blurted out the first words that came to her mind. "I'd get a whipping with a birch rod if I lost it."

"Reckon you would," Mr. Murdock said. "Makes me think of my father. He cut a hole in the bottom of a loaf of bread and put his money inside. That was a stupid thing. Anyone could see where the hole was."

Ellen was glad the snuffbox had been put in the dough and baked inside. There was nothing that would show in case he wanted to look at it.

Ten

"Hold back the night! Hold back the night!" Ellen said over and over as they rode along. She watched the trees stand black against the dull red sunset. Slowly the sky faded into gray and then turned into night.

She thought anxiously of Mr. Shannon's courier and wondered how long he would wait. Was he watching the few stars that came out in the wintry sky? It must be a long, long ride from Elizabeth to Pennsylvania. If the General was to have the message tomorrow, the first courier would have to start soon. Grandfather would have been there long ago, had he come.

It had grown very dark when Mr. Murdock turned his head to her and spoke over his shoulder. "It's black as pitch. You'd better sleep in the loft with my boys tonight."

"Oh, no!" cried Ellen. "I couldn't do that."

"How you going to get to Elizabeth?"

Ellen took a long breath. "Walk," she said in a very low voice.

Then she remembered the coins in her pocket.

"Mr. Murdock!" she said. "I can pay you to ride me to Elizabeth."

"We-l-l-," the farmer thought it over, but he said no more.

"I have the money," Ellen urged him. "I'll give it all to you."

"Hm-m-m. Well—"

Would he ever make up his mind!

"You said it was only half a mile," she reminded him.

"We'll see what Ma says first. I have to feed my two cows in the woods and they'll be bellowing to be milked. Then I have to round up my pigs and tie them up."

"And then could we start?" asked Ellen.

"Well, Ma will be mighty mad if we don't sit down to her supper. Ma gets mad easy. But I reckon I can take you when I get through."

Perhaps, Ellen thought, she'd better hurry on by herself. After all the trouble she had had today, it would be terrible if she missed the courier. But when she heard the lonesome howl of an animal far away she changed her mind. Surely the courier would not start this early. "It won't be so late," she kept assuring herself.

She could smell the wood smoke from the chimney before she saw the shadowy house near the road. It, too, was tightly closed with no light showing from the windows.

"Well, we're here," said Mr. Murdock as he turned through the gate.

He tied the horse to a ring in the wall. "Open up! I'm home again," he shouted. The door was flung wide and two young boys ran out. In the dim light Ellen could see a big black pig tied by his hind leg to a stake just outside the door.

"Oh, Pa," the boys shouted as they gathered up the baskets. "We found this mean old pig in the woods and tied him up."

"Good," said the farmer. "We'll turn him into

pork tomorrow."

A tall lanky woman came to the door and held it open for them. Her eyes were angry and her face, beneath a ruffled white cap, looked as if it were hacked out of gray stone. She bounced a crying baby on her hip and slapped at a toddler tugging at her drooping skirt.

"You're back at last!" she snapped.

And then to Ellen's surprise she burst into tears. "Thank the Lord for that," she said as she roughly brushed her tears away with the back of her hand.

Ellen followed Mr. Murdock and the boys into the house. The woman did not seem to see her. She was scolding her husband as she hurried to the fireplace and picked up a big spoon.

"In times like these it ain't safe to ride to Amboy to sell leather. If you're dead I got these four boys to raise."

"The bootmaker paid me and we need the money." Mr. Murdock lifted his yellow beard and took some money from the bag that hung from a cord about his neck. "Nothing to be worried about."

"Worried!" cried his wife in a high shrill voice. "With all those redcoats around?"

She banged her spoon as she stirred the pot of stew

that hung over the fire. Her voice became low and firm. "Times were better before the war started. That's what I think."

"Now, Ma, don't talk like that."

Mr. Murdock pushed Ellen forward, but his wife paid her no mind.

As she stood waiting for the farmer's wife to notice her, Ellen looked around the log farmhouse. The whole house was just one big shadowy room lighted by a fire on the hearth at one side. Pots and ladles and kettles of iron hung on hooks near the fireplace. In one corner stood a huge spinning wheel and in another corner a big unmade bed with a trundle bed beneath it and a cradle beside it. When she saw that a ladder went up through a dark hole to the boys' beds in the loft, Ellen was glad she wasn't going to spend the night in that cold place.

Mistress Murdock was still upset as she put wooden bowls and earthen mugs on the table. "I said times were better before the war started. Everything was peaceful, and we farmed our farm and no soldiers bothered us." She banged the pitcher of milk on the table. "I say King George was all right. He didn't bother us none. Why do we want to change things?"

Mr. Murdock pushed Ellen toward the fire. He

seemed to want to change the subject.

"I brought home a boy named Toliver who's mighty hungry."

Ellen remembered to snatch off her cap and stuff it in her pocket before she nodded her head politely as a boy would have done.

The farmer's wife looked at her glumly. Then she looked into the pot of stew and gave it a quick stir. "There's enough," she said, "if he ain't too hungry. Pa, go out and hide your horse in the woods. Supper has waited long enough."

With his wooden milk pail in his hand, Mr. Murdock quickly pulled his cap over his bushy hair, hunched his shoulders and stomped out the door.

"Boys!" Mistress Murdock ordered, "Go help your Pa." She pulled a bench up to the fire. "Sit," she said to Ellen.

Ellen hadn't known how hungry she was until she smelled that pot of stew—meat and onions and turnips. What a wonderful supper for someone who hadn't eaten anything but oatcakes since early morning.

She stuffed her mittens in one of her pockets and carefully untied the blue bundle. "This bread can dry out here by the fire while I eat supper. It's my grand-father's loaf of bread," she explained to Mistress Murdock. "It fell in the water."

The woman looked at it. "It's right soggy," she said. "Not good for much!" She picked up the wet kerchief and spread it out to dry on a pile of firewood.

"Your feet are soggy, too," she said as she bent down to look at Ellen's shoes. "And your breeches! Faith! You're wet to the skin!" she cried, wiping her hands on her apron. "Take off those breeches, Toliver," she ordered. "We'll hang them by the fire, too."

Take off her breeches? And risk that woman finding out she was a girl? Ellen was alarmed. How could she explain why she was dressed as a boy? Only spies and criminals went around pretending to be someone else.

"Oh, no!" she cried in dismay. "I'm going to Elizabeth-town tonight."

"Elizabeth!" The woman stared at her. "Tonight? In the dark—and in this kind of weather! You'd freeze to death!"

"But I must go! Mr. Murdock said he'd ride me there."

"Ride you to Elizabeth! On a night like this!" The farmer's wife clapped her hands to her head. "What now! That man must have lost his wits."

She gripped Ellen's shoulder roughly in her strong

hand. "Take off those breeches, boy! You're chilled to the bone. What ails you? Are you bashful?"

Ellen drew back. "Someone is waiting for me—" she began.

Suddenly the woman picked her up, tossed her on the bed and started to peel off the wet breeches. Ellen kicked her legs and tried to squirm away.

At that the woman's face went white with anger. "There will be no riding out where those soldiers are tonight!" she said through her tight lips. "If he gets shot I've got four boys to raise! So you can take off those breeches and let them dry. He's not going to Elizabeth—and neither are you."

In desperation Ellen pushed the woman's hands away and, grabbing the top of her breeches and kicking her feet, she worked her way to the edge of the bed. Mistress Murdock stepped back and looked at her. "What's wrong with you, Toliver?" she cried.

Quickly Ellen scrambled from the bed and ran for the door. She was glad to find it was not bolted. She flung it open and darted out into the night, pulling up her breeches as she ran. Thank goodness she had not yet taken off her jacket or shoes.

She flew through the gate and across the road and

hid among the trees. It was not until the door swung closed and all was dark around her that she remembered.

The loaf of bread. She had left it on the hearth.

A wild fright came over her as she stood shivering in the dark cold night. What could she do now? She couldn't tell Mr. Murdock. He was suspicious about the bread anyway. And she couldn't go back to the door. That stubborn woman might take away all her clothes and give her a cornmeal sack for a nightdress.

She was shaking with cold and fear and anger. How could she have forgotten the bread that she had guarded so carefully all day? How could she have been so stupid?

Then a square of light broke into the darkness and there stood Mistress Murdock in the open doorway. "Here, pig," the woman said as she flung Ellen's loaf to the pig. "Turn that soggy old bread into pork!" The door slammed shut and all was dark again.

Ellen could hear the pig grunt and snuffle around. When he found the bread he would gulp it quickly, and in his greediness he would swallow the snuffbox, too.

Ellen was afraid of pigs. She always walked clear of those lean hungry public pigs who wandered about the New York streets and ate the garbage. She remembered the mean look of the pig who had chased her this morning.

But now there wasn't a second to lose. She had to get the bread. She could feel her kneecaps shaking and she couldn't make them stop as she raced across the road. If only there was more light from the pale stars overhead. She put out her hands to grope for the pig's prickly back and when she felt it she ran her fingers down to his lowered head. But the thought of his sharp teeth made her snatch them away. The smell of him—the awful smell of him made her gag.

Again she reached out her hands. He rumbled in his throat and gave her a shove with his hips. She ran her hands along his back again and he snorted angrily. Now her eyes had grown used to the dark and she could tell that the bread was already in his mouth. She must grab for it. There was nothing else to do.

Quickly she snatched her cap from her pocket and swished it across his eyes, back and forth across his eyes. The pig tossed his head and snorted in rage. It was a terrifying sound! But when Ellen saw the bread fall from his mouth she scooped it up quickly and darted out of his way. She was glad he was tied to the stake and couldn't charge her.

As she raced through the gate and down the road, her feet barely touched the ground. She heard the door open and Mistress Murdock call out, "You all right, Pa? You got the boys there with you?" But Ellen didn't turn to look.

Mistress Murdock couldn't see her running down the road, for she was out of sight with the loaf of bread in her trembling arms. She knew Grandfather's snuffbox was safe inside. She could feel with her fingers that there was only one bite gone and not a very big bite at that. Since she had no kerchief to wrap around it she tucked it up under her jacket where it sat like a lump of ice on her stomach.

Eleven

And now there was only a half mile to go. Mr.
Murdock had said that his house was only a half mile
from Elizabeth-town. But how in the world could she
ever walk on legs that were shaking like saplings in
a windstorm? And how could she ever find her way
in the great loneliness of the night? She could hardly
see the road at all. It was only the rough hoof-marks
of horses that had passed by that helped her feet find
the way.

She stumbled along choking down the fear that

made a lump in her chest. "I fought a pig," she kept telling herself, "so I can do this, too."

On either side of the road the trees stood black against the dark sky. It seemed to her that their branches were arms—moving, groaning, bending low to grab her. She tried to remember the friendly look of the trees in the late afternoon light. But these were more frightening. Each hair seemed to stand up straight on her head, and she put on her cap to hold them down.

"They're only the trees and they can't hurt me," she said over and over. "And that moaning sound— it's only the wind." With sharp lashes, it whipped angrily around her cold wet legs.

Ellen was all alone but she was filled with a stubborn will. Nothing was going to stop her now that she was only half a mile from Mr. Shannon's tavern.

Whenever she passed a dark shadow of a farmhouse sitting behind a stone wall, she could smell the smoke from the chimney. There must be people inside. People eating bowls of piping hot stew, sitting beside a crackling fire. Perhaps children were pulling on nightshirts that had been warmed at the fire. Perhaps they were climbing into bed and putting their feet against warm bricks wrapped in wool. Mother had always warmed her bed for her this way at home.

Not a crack of light showed at the windows. Although a dog barked at the sound of her feet crunching in the snow, the doors remained shut.

And then, far ahead, she saw a light no bigger than a needle prick in the dark.

"Maybe it's Mr. Shannon's tavern!" she cried, and tried to run. But her cold wet feet would not obey her. They stumbled and slid on the frozen road and she could not make them hurry.

As she slipped from one uneven hoof mark to the next, she found herself saying over and over, "I shall run and not faint: I shall walk and not grow weary." Somehow, the words made her think of Grandfather. She remembered him sitting by the fire in the kitchen with his little reading glasses on his nose and the old Dutch Psalm Book in his hands. "They that wait upon the Lord," she could hear her grandfather's cheerful voice, "they shall walk and not be weary: they shall run and not faint." It made her feel better to think of the words that Grandfather read aloud and believed so firmly.

When at last she came close to the light she saw that it poured from an open doorway. She knew it was the doorway of a blacksmith's shop by the clang of a hammer on an iron anvil. Wearily she stumbled up to the door and leaned against the doorframe. When she could catch her breath she would ask the smith the way to the Jolly Fox Tavern.

The small barn was filled with dark shadows and flickering lights, for at one side the fire in the fireplace glowed on a hearth that was almost as high as a table. How good it was to feel the warm air blow over her as she stepped inside.

The blacksmith was startled when he looked up from the anvil where he was beating a horseshoe into shape. His blue eyes shown bright in his grimy face.

"What brings you here, boy?" he said sharply. "It's a cold night to be out."

"Oh, sir, I'm frozen into an icicle."

"Step up to the fire, then, but don't alarm the horse."

Ellen ran up to the fireplace just as the smith raised a dirty hand and pulled the rope of a huge leather bellows. A burst of air from its small mouth sent a swirl of sparks flying up among the shadows and made the fire flare up in a bright flame. The whole soot-covered room was filled with light. From the rafters overhead hung old iron tools and worn-out bits of harness and broken yokes for oxen. Even the brick fireplace looked old covered with a coat of sooty cobwebs.

With the barn brightened by the fire, Ellen could see at the other side of the room an old gray horse waiting to be shod. And in the corner beside the horse a big man sitting on a barrel. He was wearing a plaid muffler wrapped around his fur hat and tied across his mouth. He saluted her with one mittened hand and held the reins of the horse in the other. He said nothing, but she could feel his sharp eyes look at her closely.

"Maybe he's the courier," she said to herself. "But no—not with that old horse. A courier would have a strong, swift horse who could run for hours."

When the smith lifted his long tongs and put the horseshoe into the fire, the hairs on his arms shone like copper and matched the lock of hair that fell over his forehead.

"Where did you come from?" he asked.

"Oh-h-h—" Ellen hesitated. She was so cold and miserable she could not think of an answer.

"Never saw you before. Where you from?"

"From—" Ellen groped for some kind of answer. "From—from Mr. Murdock's farm."

"You a bound boy there?" asked the man in the fur hat. Ellen jumped and turned to see him pull the muffler down from his mouth. He had tipped his head to one side and was watching her carefully.

The blacksmith grunted. "I'll wager that wife of his would send a boy out on a night like this. She's a strange woman—Mistress Murdock." He began beating the curved piece of red-hot iron with his hammer.

"Will you tell me the way—" Ellen began.

Suddenly the horse stamped his feet on the wooden floor and the big man jumped up and patted his nose and rubbed his ears to quiet him. He was the tallest man Ellen had ever seen.

As she waited for the man to quiet his horse, she took off her mittens, leaned forward and held out her cold hands to the fire. She quickly clutched her jacket when she felt the loaf of bread start to slip down.

"What's that under your coat?" the big man spoke up quickly.

"It's nothing," said Ellen.

"Must be a sack of gold," he said. "Do you think it is a sack of gold, Smithy?" Ellen looked to see if he were serious, but she could not tell.

"No," said the smith, "but I'll wager it's a bag of good English coins."

"Perhaps he's a paymaster for the redcoats," said the big man.

"Or a runaway thief."

Ellen thought they must be teasing her. She looked from one face to the other. The smith was serious. The other man's eyes were laughing. She hugged the bread close to her chest.

It seemed to her the tall man's eyes looked right past the brass buttons of her coat. She was sure he could see the loaf of bread underneath. But she was not going to show it to him.

"Did you steal something from the redcoats?" he asked as he leaned forward and peered at her across the room. Perhaps he wasn't teasing after all.

The smith grumbled. "Lots of stealing around here —horses—saddles—blankets. You can't trust anyone these days. Not since the British came. Now bring up the horse," he said to the man with the muffler.

Ellen backed into the corner on the far side of the fireplace while the old horse was led to the blacksmith's side and tied to the wall.

"My horse is too old for any redcoat to steal," said the owner. He patted the horse's nose while the smith lifted a hind leg and steadied it on the leather apron that covered his knees. With a sharp knife he began to slice off small bits of the hoof before he attached the iron shoe.

"Now," said the man in the muffler, "what's under your jacket, boy?"

"Nothing," cried Ellen. "Nothing at all."

"It must be right valuable," said the man, "from the way you are hiding it."

"It's nothing but a loaf of bread," Ellen called over her shoulder as she dodged around him and darted to the door. She almost choked over the words, she was so tired and upset. Maybe they were only teasing her, but she wasn't sure. She did not know who this tall man was or why he was so curious about what was under her jacket, but she had had enough trouble for today. She did not need any more.

Twelve

She was out in the cold black night again. And now there was no spot of light ahead to give her courage to push on. Everything had gone wrong today. Over and over again! She was so miserable she wanted to sink down in the snow and go to sleep.

She heard some horsemen come galloping down the road and quickly dodged out of the way. She could not see them as they disappeared in the dark, but she could hear them round a bend in the road ahead and then suddenly stop. Far away she heard a burst of laughter, as if a door had been opened and closed again.

"That might be the tavern!" It was almost too much to hope for, but it made sense. It might be the tavern.

When she came to the bend, she saw a group of horses tied to a long hitching post. A light from a small lantern in a window shone on a sign over the doorway.

It was the picture of a smiling fox. The Jolly Fox Tavern at last! She had found it.

Ellen pushed open the door and stumbled into a room that seemed to be bouncing with laughter and singing. It smelled of hot food and old ale and muddy boots. Candles on the tables and a crackling fire in a huge fireplace made the room glow.

Sprawled on chairs around the long tables were many red-coated officers. They smoked their white pipes, banged their mugs on the bare boards and joked with two nimble waitresses in white caps and long green aprons.

Beside the fireplace at the far end of the room Ellen saw a bar with slats of wood from counter to ceiling. She had never been in a tavern before and had never seen a little room like this. It looked like a cage. The shelves at the back were filled with wine bottles and mugs and pewter tankards. White clay tobacco pipes hung from the rafters overhead, waiting to be borrowed by the customers.

Inside the cage a plump little woman was drawing ale from a keg into a row of mugs. She, too, wore a long green apron. And in her ears were gold earrings that sparkled when she turned her head in time to the tune she was whistling. A small British flag was stuck jauntily in her white topknot. "Is this Mistress Shannon?" Ellen wondered.

She ran up to her and asked cautiously, "May I speak to Mr. Shannon?"

The little white-haired woman pushed four mugs along the counter and called to a waitress, "Don't keep the gentlemen waiting." Then she turned to Ellen. "What's your pleasure, sir?" She threw back her head and started to laugh. "You're about as small as they come," she chuckled.

"May I see Mr. Shannon?" Ellen asked again. She was impatient because the woman was so slow. Now that she was here she wanted to thrust the bread into Mr. Shannon's hands. Who was this woman with the British flag in her white hair?

The woman started singing in a loud voice as she wiped her hands on the towel at her waist. Her eyes darted quickly about the room as she leaned forward and put her head through the gateway of her cage. "Mr. Shannon's not here," she said.

"Not here!" Ellen was filled with dismay.

"He has gone to the country to find a few kegs of ale."

"Gone!" cried Ellen in a voice that was sharp and frightened. What did she mean, gone? Grandfather said he would be here! Waiting for her!

"When will he be back?" she asked desperately.

The woman was banging mugs on the counter and making a great clatter with some dishes. "In a day or two. No telling when." She seemed to be looking past Ellen at the soldiers in the room.

"I have come a long way—" Ellen began. But the woman's loud singing drowned out her words.

When she could interrupt her, Ellen pleaded, "—and I must find him—now. Can you help me?"

"He's gone to the country," the woman said again in a very loud voice, "to find some more ale for these thirsty men. No telling which way he went."

Then she leaned across the counter and whispered, "Just sit by the fire, boy." Her face was filled with friendly concern. "Just close your eyes and don't talk to anyone at all. I'm Mr. Shannon's wife."

And with that she went back to the keg of ale,

picking up the song the soldiers were singing, and shouting it as lustily as they. The little flag fluttered with each toss of her head.

Ellen wanted to give Mistress Shannon the loaf of bread, and be done with it. But she remembered her grandfather's warning. "Give the bread to no one but Mr. Shannon."

Two redcoats moved their outstretched legs to make way for her as she stumbled over to the fire and sat down on a low stool. On a spit before the fire a roast of mutton was sizzling and sputtering. But not even the smell of a good hot roast made her hungry. She was too tired and upset and numb with shock.

As she watched the leaping flames, her head whirled with memories of the day. They went past her eyes in a dizzy parade—the boat full of soldiers, the crowded streets of Amboy, the woods, that awful pig! And for what? For nothing! Mr. Shannon wasn't here! All that she had endured meant nothing in the end! She could sit here and wait all she liked, Mr. Shannon wouldn't be back for two days.

Angrily she kicked off her wet shoes and shoved them toward the fire. She leaned forward, doubling up over the loaf of bread inside her jacket, put her head on her knees, and let her arms flop down. She was too tired to move. The noise of the tavern swirled about her, but Ellen barely heard it.

Before long she felt a tap on her shoulder and saw the woman with the flag in her hair beckoning to her. Very slowly she got up. "I don't think she's really Mistress Shannon. She's too friendly with the redcoats," Ellen said to herself. But she hugged the loaf of bread under her jacket and followed her, just the same.

They passed the bar and quietly slipped into a room at the back. The woman locked the door behind them. It was a small room, lighted only by a fire of pine knots and rather crowded with a large bed in one corner and two big chairs by the fireplace. The heavy red curtains at the windows were tightly drawn.

In the dim light Ellen saw a man rise from one of the chairs. To her surprise, she recognized the tall man in the fur hat and the plaid muffler. His eyes were grave as he pulled the muffler from his long chin.

"You're a quick one," he said. "You ran away too fast." When he unwound the muffler and took off his hat, his thick white hair fell to his shoulders.

Ellen liked his face, now that she could see it clearly. It was a strong face with a good wide mouth and ruddy cheeks. She remembered his eyes under his white eyebrows. They had seemed to bore through her jacket in the blacksmith shop, but now they were smiling. He was so tall and rugged he made her think of a great oak tree in the woods.

"This is Mr. Shannon," whispered the woman. "He has come back sooner than I expected."

Was he really Mr. Shannon? Ellen wondered. How could she be sure? She thought Mr. Shannon would be a round and jolly innkeeper in a long green apron. She thought he might look like her grandfather, since they were good friends. And why would Mr. Shannon go after ale for the soldiers if he were expecting an important message? And that woman who said she was his wife was wearing a little British flag in her hair. It was rather odd.

"Is that a loaf of bread you are hiding in your jacket?" Mr. Shannon said.

"Yes-s-s," Ellen answered slowly.

"Is it a present for my birthday?"

"Yes, it is," she cried in surprise.

"From Van Horn, the barber in New York?"

Now she was sure. Only Mr. Shannon would know about her grandfather.

"Here it is, Mr. Shannon!" she said eagerly as she slipped the loaf of bread from her jacket. Standing

there in her stocking feet, she curtsied as she handed him the bread and said the words she had carried in her mind all day. "I have brought you a present for your birthday." Then she added, "My grandfather hurt his ankle this morning and he couldn't walk at all. So he sent me."

As she gave the loaf of bread to Mr. Shannon she felt as if a great load had been lifted from her shoulders. She had delivered Grandfather's message! In spite of everything, she had delivered the message! Her face was beaming.

"But how did you get here from New York?" Mr. Shannon looked puzzled. "You were walking, weren't you, when you came into the smithy?"

"I had to walk part of the way," Ellen told him.

"Not from Amboy!" he exclaimed. "You couldn't have walked from Amboy!"

"Oh, I got a ride partway with Mr. Murdock. Most of the way. He was going to ride me all of the way, but—"

Mr. Shannon interrupted her. "How in the world did you get to Amboy?"

"On a British boat. A soldier—"

"On a British boat!" He stared at her in disbelief.

"It was because some boys stole my bread in New

York and made me so late I missed the farmers' boats."

"But how did you get on a British boat?"

"Oh, a man grabbed me. He wanted my loaf of bread."

Mr. Shannon stared at her in amazement. "And you worked your way through all those troubles to get the bread here to me! Well, we're very grateful to you, son!"

Ellen looked up at this very tall man who had charge of relaying the message to the night-riding couriers. He was smiling at her. She felt like telling him that she really had been scared all the time. But a man like Mr. Shannon wouldn't understand about being afraid.

"I'd like to stay and have supper with you," he said, "but people are waiting to take this message on its way. Three different couriers will carry it across New Jersey and deliver it tomorrow. So I must hurry to give it to the first man, who lives not far from here."

As he tied the bread in his own blue kerchief, he said, "Lucky it was that my horse threw a shoe when I started out to look for your grandfather. I got to thinking about you—there in the smithy—and I decided I'd better come back to see if you stopped here."

Mistress Shannon hugged his arm to her cheek and

opened the door to the dark night. A cold gust of wind made her skirts billow out. "Be very cautious," she said with concern. "There are redcoats everywhere." After she had bolted the door she hurried to the hearth and poked at the fire until it blazed up enough to brighten the room. She pulled a small log from a box and added it to the fire.

When she turned to Ellen she was smiling. She put her hands on her shoulders and looked into her eyes. "Now tell me your real name, young lady!"

"Why," cried Ellen in surprise, "I'm a—"

Mistress Shannon put her arms around her. "Never did I see a boy make such a pretty curtsy as you made a few minutes ago."

Ellen gasped. Had she curtsied? How could she have been so stupid? It must have been her stocking feet that made her forget her disguise.

"I—just—don't know—" she stammered.

Mistress Shannon's eyes were shining proudly as she looked at her. "Tell me your name?" she begged.

"Well," Ellen admitted, since there was no reason to be secret any longer, "my name is Ellen—Ellen Toliver."

Mistress Shannon chuckled. And then she burst out

laughing and quickly covered her mouth with her hands.

"Oh, the things we do to fool those redcoats," she giggled. "All day long I pretend I'm a loyal subject of the King—out there in the tavern singing away like a bird in a cage. And you pretend you're a boy with nothing but a loaf of bread in your kerchief."

She patted Ellen's cheeks playfully. "But we fool them, don't we, Ellen? And we get important messages through the lines to our army."

Ellen felt so good and so relieved, thinking how she fooled everyone, she began to laugh. She was carried away by such gales of laughter she had to stuff the green apron in her mouth to keep from being heard in the taproom. She felt silly with the apron in her mouth, but she just could not stop. Every time they looked at each other—the plump little woman with a flag in her white hair, and the girl in leather breeches and a boy's jacket—they burst out laughing again.

Mistress Shannon took time to bring Ellen a hot potpie from the kitchen to eat in front of the fire. Then she brought a mug of warm milk. And next a shawl to wrap about her legs after she had hung her stockings by the fire. Every time she came back, Ellen told her more of the story—about Dow and his eagerness to eat the bread, and the pig, and how Mistress Murdock almost stole her breeches.

Now that she was safe, Ellen could hardly believe the things she told Mistress Shannon. They seemed so far away already. Suddenly she could hardly hold her eyes open. Mistress Shannon pulled a trundle bed from under the big bed and put a heavy blanket on it. She gave Ellen one of her nightgowns and a nightcap, and bustled about the room, carefully spreading out Ellen's clothes to dry.

"You are snug and safe now, Ellen," she said softly. "We'll send you back home early in the morning."

Ellen fell heavily into the comfortable bed. Sleep came so quickly she barely heard Mistress Shannon call to her from the doorway, "You've earned a good night's rest, Ellen Toliver."

Thirteen

*L*ong before sunrise, Mistress Shannon brought Ellen's dry clothes to her. The shoes were still wet, but her feet would be snug in an extra pair of woolen stockings.

"No more adventures today, Ellen," she said as she stirred up a good fire and put a breakfast of hot porridge and sausages on the table.

Mr. Shannon came in and sat beside Ellen while she ate. "The courier left last night, Ellen," he told her, "with the bread in his saddlebag. By now, the second courier should be near the third man. It takes a chain of people to carry a message across the country-side quickly."

"It's dangerous, isn't it," said Ellen, "to ride through enemy country?"

"Well," he admitted, "it is dangerous. But it's no more dangerous than fighting in the army. I'm too old to fight. Most of us are old men—or women who carry messages sewn in their clothes—or boys, too young to fight." He leaned over and patted her arm as he smiled at her. "Or a girl like you! Your link in the chain didn't break, Ellen. We're all glad about that."

It was worth going through all the troubles of yesterday to hear him say that.

Mr. Shannon carried a burning torch to light their way to the little river that went from Elizabeth to the Bay half a mile away. At the dock several boats were being loaded with barrels of food for the market-house in New York.

"We'll send you home with Grimsby who is our good friend," said Mr. Shannon. "He's taking a big load of Christmas greens to town."

"But when the war is over," Mistress Shannon added, "we hope you'll come back for a peaceful visit to Elizabeth. Will you come and bring your grandfather?"

"Oh, yes," Ellen promised. "You may be sure of that." She felt the Shannons were her good friends.

Mr. Shannon spoke to the two leather-faced sailors, "Take good care of this youngster. This is a very special person."

Grimsby and Gallop made a seat for her among the bundles of pine and spruce boughs. "There's a brisk breeze this morning," they told her while they covered her legs with greens. "Won't take long to get back to New York."

The sky grew pink and the torches sputtered out. They were off. In no time the boat sailed down the little river past the swampy marshes and the big wharves at the shore. It was not long before Ellen recognized the shoreline of Staten Island. "Why, we sailed past here yesterday," she said to herself. "We must have been quite near Elizabeth before we sailed on to Perth Amboy." She shrugged her shoulders the way Grandfather sometimes shrugged his. "But I never would have seen how the enemy is getting ready in Perth Amboy. Mr. Shannon wanted me to tell him about that."

The day turned out to be a cheerful one with a great arch of blue sky and a bright sun overhead. Not at all like yesterday—except for the men's singing. Ellen liked to listen to the songs Grimsby and Gallop sang while they handled the sails and the tiller of the old boat.

"Sing right up, boy," Grimsby called to her. "Oh, my name is Captain Kidd, who has sailed, who has sailed—" he sang out.

Ellen sang the refrain. "Who has sailed, who has sailed."

At first she sang the refrains in a small voice. And then in a loud one as she began to enjoy the sound of her singing—even though she didn't understand some of the words.

They sang "On the Banks of the Dee" and "Yankee Doodle" and "The Revolutionary Tea." It was exciting to sing Yankee songs as they sailed past the British ships anchored near the shores of Staten Island.

Ellen was standing by the mast singing at the top of her voice when their scow sailed up the East River and wound its way among the boats that were anchored there. Snow lay white on the roofs of the gabled houses and the sun glinted from the church spires.

"New York looks good," she said to Grimsby, and she meant it.

Grimsby and Gallop waved to her as she hopped off the boat. She staggered about the dock until she got used to walking on land, while they stood and laughed. Then she took off her cap and waved to them.

Soon she was running along the street and pushing her way through the crowds. They were the same crowds as yesterday—the same noisy men with wheelbarrows, the same rowdy boys, the same grumbling workmen with heavy loads on their backs. But she felt different. She wasn't afraid of them. They were all going about their affairs—just as she was. She ran in and out of the crowds, laughing to herself. She wasn't a rabbit any more.

She felt like singing as she climbed up the steps and burst into her grandfather's shop. She pushed past two British officers and past her grandfather's shaver, Alexander, who had a big bowl of soapsuds in his hand. She was so happy to be home she would have smiled at the leeches if she had thought to. Grandfather's face lighted up when he saw her. Rising from his couch he hopped after her to the kitchen and locked the door behind him.

"I did it!" Ellen cried in a loud whisper as she kicked off her shoes and danced about the room. "I did it! I did it!" She grabbed her mother's hands and they whirled around together while Grandfather waved the crutch the carpenters had made him. He would have danced, too, if he had had two feet.

Over and over they hugged her and said, "We're so happy you are home." Pulling chairs up to the big table by the window, they sat down to hear about her trip.

"You found the farmers' boats without trouble?" Grandfather asked in a whisper.

"Trouble!" Ellen groaned. "I had nothing but trouble. Trouble all day long."

Mother and Grandfather looked at her in surprise. They could hardly believe the whispered tale she told them.

"Perth Amboy was filled with cannon and wagon trains and hundreds of soldiers," said Ellen. "Mr. Shannon told me that General Cornwallis was there in Perth Amboy getting ready to finish off our army before winter sets in."

"That's what we feared," said Grandfather gravely. "But you did get the message to Mr. Shannon, didn't you?"

"Yes, I did," said Ellen, "and now I understand why it is so important for couriers to take messages to our army."

"I had no idea it would be so hard for you, Ellen," Grandfather said. "I don't know whether I would have sent you had I known. But I, myself, never would have been able to get through the lines at all. No one would have smuggled a fat old man on a boat." His eyes twinkled.

Mother leaned across the table and smiled at her. "I'm proud of you, Ellen," she whispered. "But I hope you'll never have to do it again."

"Well," said Ellen as she thought that over, "I think maybe I'd do it again . . . I don't know . . . I guess I'd do it again if the boat was sure to go to Elizabeth-town."

It seemed to Ellen that two good things happened to her after her trip to New Jersey. The first happened the next morning when she wrapped her red cloak around her and went to the pump early. Ellen took her place at the end of the line to wait her turn. The women were still talking about the high price of food and the high price of firewood. It seemed to Ellen she had been away a hundred years—and they were still talking about the same old things.

Then Dicey came by. Her face grew red with anger when she saw Ellen.

"Are you here again?" she cried as she walked slowly, heavily toward Ellen.

"Yes, I'm here again!" Ellen put down her bucket. She was ready to duck out of the way if Dicey came too close. But she was not afraid of her. She folded her arms across her chest.

Dicey growled, "I told you not to come here, Miss Fine Lady."

Ellen thrust out her chin and stared back at Dicey. "This pump is near my house," she said calmly. "And I intend to use it, no matter what you say."

Dicey stared back, but she came no further. For almost half a minute they stared at each other. Then Dicey shrugged and turned away.

"You're just lucky I'm not ready for a fight," she called over her shoulder. But she walked away.

The second good thing happened a month later. Grandfather's silver snuffbox came back to him by way of a secret courier. In it was a message that gave them wonderful news.

General Washington's small army had crossed the Delaware River from Pennsylvania to New Jersey on

Christmas night and had taken the city of Trenton by surprise. Washington had been able to plan a surprise attack because he had learned so much about British plans from the Patriots in New York and the couriers who had carried their messages.

Then he and his army had moved on to another victory at Princeton early in January and had time to fortify winter headquarters in Morristown behind the Watchung Hills in New Jersey.

And there was news of Ezra Toliver. He was a sergeant now and was safe and well in Morristown. They hugged one another for joy when they heard that.

In the snuffbox there was also a folded piece of paper marked, "For Toliver." To Ellen's surprise she found inside a tiny silver locket. She never knew who sent it to her, but since she didn't know she liked to pretend it was from the General himself. And who knows—perhaps it was.

Esther Wood Brady

was born in Akron, New York, and raised in New York and Ohio. As a young woman she traveled around the world by freighter, spending time in remote parts of China, Japan, and the Philippines. In addition to raising a family and writing, Mrs. Brady has worked in public schools tutoring children with reading difficulties. She now lives with her husband in Washington, D.C. TOLIVER'S SECRET is her first book for Crown.

Richard Cuffari,

illustrator of numerous books for children, was born in Brooklyn and is a graduate of Pratt Institute. His work has been selected for an AIGA Children's Books Show and has appeared many times in the annual exhibits of the Society of Illustrators. He lives in Brooklyn, New York, with his children.

J
BRA

Brady, Esther Wood

Toliver's secret

77-179

DATE